A legendary creatu

MW01536607

When a satellite photograph reveals the location of a legendary lost city deep in the Congo River basin, journalist Mackenzie Moore knows it is only a matter of time before its secrets are revealed to the world. In order to get there first, she needs someone capable and crazy enough to take her there.

Treasure hunter and former Navy SEAL Bones Bonebrake loves adventure and hates boredom. But an expedition into one of the world's most dangerous and remote locations might turn out to be more than he bargained for. Somewhere in the depths of the Dark Continent lies Mbanza Mpimpá, the City of Night. But this seemingly abandoned city does not surrender its secrets easily, and intruders are not welcome in the *Lost City*!

Classic adventure for the modern reader! Fans of Indiana Jones, Dirk Pitt, and National Treasure will love the Bones Bonebrake Adventures!

Praise for David Wood

"Jurassic Park meets Jungle Cruise in this rollicking adventure!" Rick Chesler, author of *Golden One*

"What an adventure! A great read that provides lots of action, and thoughtful insight as well, into strange realms that are sometimes best left unexplored." Paul Kemprecos, author of *Cool Blue Tomb* and the *NUMA Files*

LOST CITY

A Bones Bonebrake Adventure

DAVID WOOD

MATT JAMES

Lost City- ©2020 by David Wood

The Bones Bonebrake Adventures are a part of the Dane
Maddock ™ universe!

Published by Adrenaline Press
www.adrenaline.press

Adrenaline Press is an imprint of Gryphonwood Press
www.gryphonwoodpress.com

ISBN: 9798681098584

Books and Series by David Wood

The Dane Maddock Adventures
Blue Descent
Dourado
Cibola
Quest
Icefall
Buccaneer
Atlantis
Ark
Xibalba
Loch
Solomon Key
Contest
Serpent (forthcoming)

Dane and Bones Origins
Freedom
Hell Ship
Splashdown
Dead Ice
Liberty
Electra
Amber
Justice
Treasure of the Dead
Bloodstorm

Adventures from the Dane Maddock Universe
Berserk
Maug
The Elementals
Cavern
Devil's Face

Brainwash
Herald
The Tomb
Shasta
Destination-Rio
Destination-Luxor
Destination-Sofia

Jade Ihara Adventures (with Sean Ellis)
Oracle
Changeling
Exile

Bones Bonebrake Adventures
Primitive
The Book of Bones
Skin and Bones
Lost City

Jake Crowley Adventures (with Alan Baxter)
Sanctum
Blood Codex
Anubis Key
Revenant

Brock Stone Adventures
Arena of Souls
Track of the Beast (forthcoming)

Myrmidon Files (with Sean Ellis)
Destiny
Mystic

Sam Aston Investigations (with Alan Baxter)
Primordial

Overlord

Stand-Alone Novels
Into the Woods (with David S. Wood)
Callsign: Queen (with Jeremy Robinson)
Dark Rite (with Alan Baxter)

David Wood writing as David Debord

The Absent Gods Trilogy
The Silver Serpent
Keeper of the Mists
The Gates of Iron

The Impostor Prince (with Ryan A. Span)
Neptune's Key
The Zombie-Driven Life
You Suck

Books and Series by Matt James

JACK REILLY ADVENTURES
The Forgotten Fortune (2020)

STAND-ALONE TITLES
The Dragon
Dark Island
Sub-Zero
Cradle of Death

DANE MADDOCK ADVENTURES w/David Wood
Berserk
Skin and Bones
Lost City (2020)

DEAD MOON SERIES
Nightmares are Born
Home Sweet Hell
Song of Sorrow
In Memoriam

DEAD MOON SHORT STORIES
Nightmare at the Museum
Scared to Death

HANK BOYD ADVENTURES
Blood and Sand
Mayan Darkness
Babel Found
Elixir of Life

LOGAN REED THRILLERS

Plague
Evolve

OTHER STORIES
The Cursed Pharaoh
Broken Glass

From the Author

A few years ago, Matt James and I penned a short, fast-paced novella titled *Venom*, which told the story of Bones Bonebrake and Mackenzie Moore's journey into the Amazon rainforest in search of the legendary giant snake, Yacumama. It was published as a part of Amazon's Kindle Worlds program. Shortly thereafter, Kindle Worlds closed its doors.

I took that opportunity to revise and expand all the existing Kindle Worlds books prior to republishing them, but I held off on Venom. I had realized that there was a much deeper story I wanted to tell about the Yacumama Legend, one that would involve Maddock, too. (That book is titled *Serpent,* and it will be completed soon.)

That left us with a problem. What to do with *Venom*? At first, we tried to simply move the story to a different part of the world with a different creature, with the hope of preserving as much of the original text as possible. That didn't work out as we hoped. The new book took on a life of its own, and only a small fraction of *Venom* survived the rewrite. What's the same? A few characters, some sentences sprinkled throughout the middle of the book, a few details, and the general spirit of action-packed adventure.

So, if you've already read Venom, you may dive into Lost City knowing this is a brand-new story. You might experience the occasional bout of déjà vu when you come across the occasional sentence that survived the rewrite, or encounter a reimagined scene, but it will otherwise be a fresh reading experience for you!

We tried very hard to capture the classic jungle adventure spirit. I listened to the old radio play of *The*

African Queen and played theme music from Disney's *Jungle Cruise* ride to help me get into the spirit! It was a joy to write and we hope you love reading it as much as we did writing it.

Happy reading!

David

PROLOGUE

1920- The Congo River

"To arms! Crocodile off the starboard bow!" Edgar Arundel sprang to his feet, nearly striking his head on the canopy that covered the stern deck. He waved his arms and pointed at the riverbank. "Stand up, you layabouts! I said to arms!"

There were many English words Jafari did not know, including layabout, but he thought he understood the meaning. Lazy. Like most Europeans, Arundel had thus far sat back and let his hired hands do the work, yet still managed disdain for those in his employ.

"Do I stand or steer boat?" asked Odion, who was manning the rudder.

"Useless, both of you. When there is a call to arms, everyone obeys."

From his perch on the foredeck which covered the engine compartment, Jafari shielded his eyes from the sun and squinted in the direction of the south bank. The crocodile was sunning itself on the riverbank and appeared to have no interest in the steamboat that chugged its way up this remote tributary of the mighty Congo River.

"Is a small crocodile," Jafari said. "Not worth Sir's time."

"I will judge the value of my own time, thank you," Arundel snapped. Some of the tension seemed to leave his body.

"You take home real crocodile head to mount on wall." Jafari spread his arms wide in a V-shape like impossibly large jaws. "Giant head."

"Teeth big. Sharp." Odion drew his belt knife and held it up for emphasis.

That did the trick. Arundel nodded, rested his rifle against the gunwale, and sat back down. The man was eager to kill something, but his vanity demanded that it be a real prize. He didn't know that his hired guides had just described a creature that existed only in legends.

"Have you seen such giant crocodiles?" Arundel asked.

"Only stories," Jafari said. Of course, the creature from the stories was not exactly a crocodile. He turned away and once again focused on the river up ahead.

None of the men had ever traveled this far into the jungle before. Jafari had never so much as met someone who had plied this stretch of river. But he knew stories, and Arundel was compensating him well for this fool's errand. A lost Roman city in the jungle! Where had he gotten such a notion?

"You are certain you have heard no reports of Roman settlements in this area?" Arundel asked suddenly as if reading his thoughts.

"No Romans," Jafari said.

"Respect!" Arundel snapped. He was always taking offense at Jafari's tone or word choices. "Do not be so dismissive of my theories. It is known that the Romans explored the west coast of Africa."

Jafari didn't bother to reply. Arundel had told them all this before.

"And the Romans reached Lake Chad during the reign of Augustus. They called it 'The Lake of Hippopotamus.'"

Jafari had only heard of Lake Chad. It was a long way away. Hundreds and hundreds of miles.

"And nearly thirty years ago, a Roman coin bearing the image of the emperor Trajan was found in the Congo."

Jafari smiled and nodded. There was no point arguing with Arundel. The man was so single-minded that nothing could get him off track—not even facts or common sense. But that was often the way with people who inherited power and wealth. They simply could not be influenced by anyone they deemed lesser than themselves.

They rounded a bend and the roar of falling water drowned out Arundel's lecture. Up ahead stood a low waterfall. It was perhaps Jafari's height and no more, but it would be impossible for *Achillia* to proceed farther upriver.

"Waterfall," Jafari said. "We cannot go up."

"Nonsense," Arundel proclaimed. "We must simply portage our noble craft around the waterfall."

"Portage?" Odion repeated.

"Carry the boat between navigable waters." Arundel mimicked lifting a heavy object.

Jafari frowned. The steamboat's hull was metal, not to mention the boiler and engine. The thing would be impossible to carry.

Arundel laughed. "And now you see the benefit of a proper English education. I have come prepared. With ropes and pulleys, we can easily surmount this obstacle."

Jafari and Odion thought the man mad, but Arundel proved to know what he was doing. In short order, he had rigged an apparatus with which they were able to lift *Achillia* up and over the waterfall. Rather, the two guides had lifted the boat while Arundel supervised. By evening, they were well upriver.

The sun was setting, and night was closing in when they moored the steamboat and hiked a short distance inland to make camp. While Jafari and Odion made camp, Arundel set off into the jungle to go hunting. The guides did their best to dissuade him from heading off into the forest alone, but as expected, the arrogant adventurer dismissed their concerns.

"I am a gladiator," he said, before stalking away.

Arundel was obsessed with gladiators. From the man's many stories, Jafari inferred that Arundel was the son of an

English nobleman. He had adopted his father's fascination with Rome as a way of gaining the man's approval. He had even christened his boat with what he said was the name of a female gladiator.

They had just finished pitching the tents when thunder boomed, and heavy rain began to fall. Within minutes, it became a deluge. Neither man could see more than a few feet ahead of him.

"I should make certain the boat is secure," Odion said in their native language. He hurried away, leaving Jafari huddled beneath the shelter of their small canvas tent. Doubtless, Arundel would chastise him for not having a campfire ready, regardless of the weather.

He waited. The storm grew heavier. Neither Odion nor Arundel returned. It would soon be full dark. The river was not far. Odion, at least, should be back by now. Jafari should look for him.

He took out a small oil lantern, added fuel, and lit it using flint and steel. It cast a pitiful circle of yellow light that allowed him to see only a few paces in front of him, but it was enough that he managed to make his way back to the river.

When he got there, the boat was gone and so was Odion. He looked around to make certain he was in the right place. The raging river had overflowed its banks, but he was certain this was the way they had come. Yes! There was the tree to which they had tied off the boat.

"Odion!" he shouted again and again. No reply. Had Odion taken the boat and abandoned them? He wouldn't do that. He might leave Arundel behind, but not Jafari. They had been close since they were boys.

Something caught his notice. Part of the mooring rope was still tied to the tree. The frayed end told him that the boat had broken loose. But where was Odion?

He searched for footprints, but the rain had washed away any tracks his friend might have left. He caught sight of something flapping in a tree branch above his head. He raised his lantern and let out a curse. Odion's shirt, stained with blood, hung from the tree. How had it gotten up there, and what had happened to Odion.

He felt a sudden urge to return to camp. Perhaps Odion had made his way back. He would even welcome the sight of Arundel's face right now.

He rushed back to find the camp still empty. He was contemplating his next move when he heard gunshots in the forest nearby. There was a rustling in the brush and then Arundel came dashing into camp. He was white as a ghost.

"We have to get out of here!" the Englishman gasped. Jafari heard the sounds of something, or many somethings crashing through the jungle, coming toward them. Arundel seized his arm. "We must get to the boat."

"The boat is gone," Jafari said. "The river must have carried it away."

It was as if the life went out of Arundel. His shoulders sagged and he let his rifle fall to the ground. "Then we are truly lost," he said. In the jungle, the crashing sound came closer.

"What is that?" Jafari asked.

"That is the sound of our deaths." Arundel threw back his head and laughed.

1

The sun beat down on the muddy grassland. The fetid air reeked of stale water and decaying vegetation with a hint of dead fish. Mackenzie Moore crinkled her nose and swatted at the cloud of gnats that buzzed around her head. This swamp was home to a wealth of stinging and biting insects, poisonous snakes, and predators like the Florida Panther. The Everglades was also the only environment on the planet that could claim to be home to both alligators and crocodiles.

"James Carlos Blake was right," she said aloud. "If the devil ever raised a garden, this place would be it. So, of course this is where I have to go."

Mackenzie, whom most people called Mack, was a reporter with National Geographic. At least, she had been until Cabras. Her employer hadn't been pleased when she'd gone in search of giants and found...

Before she could finish the thought, she stepped onto what she had believed was sold ground but was, in fact, a layer of soil floating atop calf-deep water. She let out a curse as she plunged forward and landed on her hands and knees in the water and mud.

"Oh, hell no!" She made her way to dry ground and took a moment to dump the water from her boots, wring out her socks, and scrape the mud from her clothing. A ragged breeze rustled the tall grass. She resisted the urge to cover her nose. The odor reminded her of the time she was called away on a week-long business trip and returned to a load of wet laundry she had inadvertently left in the washer. "Damn you," she growled to no one in particular. "Is nothing going to go right?"

She opened her fanny pack, took out a topographical map, and tried to orient herself, but gave it up quickly. She understood the concept but didn't have the experience. Of course, that was part of the reason she was in this god-forsaken mud pit.

She took a moment to let her long, red hair down, smooth it back, and put it back up in the ponytail she preferred in most casual settings, especially in hot weather. Of course, hot did not begin to describe the Everglades.

Something moved at the corner of her eye. She turned and spotted a flash of tawny fur. She froze. It was a panther! As far as she knew, they were shy creatures who merely wanted to be left alone by humans. Still, the tension didn't leave her body until she saw the ripples in the grass that told her the creature was moving away from her. When she was sure it was gone, she breathed a deep sigh of relief.

"Toughen up, Mack," she muttered. "If you get your way, you'll be headed into much more dangerous territory than this."

Shielding her eyes against the South Florida sun, she spotted a cluster of pine and mangrove trees in the distance, like an island in a sea of grass. She smiled. That was one of her landmarks.

"Not so lost after all."

Her sense of triumph was short-lived. The intervening space was mostly water, much of it deep. She found herself winding to and fro, covering lots of ground but seemingly drawing no closer to the island of trees.

Finally, she broke through a stand of mangrove and found herself staring out at a wide mud field. If she stuck to the green space, it would mean taking a very roundabout way. She took out her phone and checked the time. Two o'clock. It had taken her an eternity to get this far. At this rate, she might not make it back before dark. And she did not want to be out here at night.

"It looks solid enough," she said, taking a tentative step forward. The ground supported her weight. "Just choose your steps carefully and you'll be fine."

It worked. She made her slow but steady way across, picking up speed as she better recognized the spots that would support her weight. But as she neared the island, the earth beneath her feet was growing softer.

"Just a bit farther." She looked up to measure the distance, and just missed stepping on a fat, black snake.

She let out a shriek and dodged to the side, startling the sunning cottonmouth. Thankfully, Mack ran one way and it slithered off in the opposite direction. Scarcely able to believe her good luck, Mack stood there, catching her breath as the snake vanished into the distant grass.

"It's about time something good happened today." Grinning, Mack headed for the pine island. Rather, she tried to, but her feet were trapped in soft mud and she was sinking fast! She tried to pull a foot free but every move she made worked her deeper into the soft earth. Hot anger cooled into something that wasn't quite fear as she tried and failed to extricate herself. What if she couldn't get herself free?

I need help, she thought. Instinctively, reaching for her phone. She stopped herself, barked a rueful laugh. She already knew she didn't have service out here. Besides, how long would it take for help to arrive, and would they be able to find her? And then an idea struck her.

The man was supposed to be somewhere near the pine island. Was it so crazy to think he might be within earshot? And what would it cost her to try?

"Help?"

It came out sounding weak. Mack was an independent sort. It wasn't in her nature to ask for help, much less scream for it. But no one was going to hear her unless she increased her volume.

"I need help out here!" She added a note of authority to it. That was better. She swallowed, growing more and more nervous as every silent second passed. Her voice caught. "Um, please somebody help me?"

She waited, listening. There was a wet, slapping sound, and something moved. But it wasn't help that was on its way.

It was a huge alligator. And it was coming right toward her.

This time, she didn't bother to modulate her tone when she cried out for help.

2

Bones Bonebrake was ready to call it a day. He had spent hours searching for clues but all he had found were snakes, mosquitoes, and dead ends. No sooner had he thought about snakes than a fast-moving cottonmouth crossed his path. Bones saw it coming and gave it a wide berth. It appeared to have no more interest in him than he in it, and the two parted ways without further conflict.

"What in the hell am I going to do for the next week?" he said to the sky. The Lost City of the Everglades was looking to be a waste of his time. His crewmates were all out of town, except for Maddock, who was holed up in his condo with the new woman in his life. He had made it clear to Bones that he was not to be disturbed until she returned home the following Sunday.

Bones enjoyed life, and aside from rednecks and the French, there weren't many things he couldn't stand, but boredom was one. The other was having no one to be bored with. He didn't exactly regret leaving the Navy SEALs for a life of treasure hunting, but at least the service had kept him occupied.

"Help?"

Bones paused. That was odd. He was certain someone had said the word "help" but she hadn't sounded like she needed help. Still, he ought to check it out, just to be safe. Keeping an eye out for more snakes, he moved through the tall grass in the direction of the sound. When he broke through, he saw a short, red-haired woman standing out in the middle of the mudflat. Check that—she was actually a tall redhead who was stuck knee-deep in the mud.

"Holy crap," he muttered. "Been there, done that." He

quickened his pace, careful not to end up in the same predicament.

"I need help out here!"

Bones grinned. The woman sounded like a drill sergeant. So that's how it was? Realistically, she had probably sunk as far as she was going to in this particular spot, but it could be a pain in the ass to get out of. And it was scary for someone who had never been stuck before. He was about to call out to her, to reassure her, but she started to scream.

"Oh my God! Somebody help me! Please!"

"Hey, calm down!" Bones shouted. "You'll just get yourself stuck deeper."

"Calm down?" she shouted. "Do you not see the giant alligator that's coming right at me?"

Bones spotted it immediately. It was huge, and it was headed right for the woman.

"You have got to be freaking kidding me." Bones took off running, hoping the earth between them would support his weight. The gator closed in on the woman, who had dug a Swiss Army Knife out of her fanny pack and was brandishing it at the giant reptile that was closing in on her. Bones admired her spirit, if not her choice of weaponry

"Don't you do it!" he shouted at the gator. He doubted it would startle the beast, but it was worth a try.

It didn't work.

"That was just great!" the redhead shouted, her voice dripping with sarcasm. "I really think you scared him."

"Do you want my help or not?" Bones huffed.

"I'd feel better if you were Steve Irwin."

"You and me both!" Bones flashed past her. He didn't dive headlong at the alligator—that would be suicide. Instead, he angled around and came in from behind.

He landed atop it and somehow got his arms around its jaw, and the powerful beast began to thrash. Bones suddenly found himself clinging to the gator's snout for dear life. If he were to let go…

He had never truly appreciated how powerful an alligator was, nor how slippery. As the beast continued to thrash around, he felt himself sliding forward. If he lost his grip, he might end up in the worst possible place—right in front of it. Gritting his teeth, he held on with all his might and worked to remain atop the gator. It was a lot like jiu-jitsu, but in this case, tapping out was not an option.

He squeezed his knees tight against its flanks, holding himself in place. Next, he worked his feet beneath its hind legs, preventing them from touching the ground, which reduced the thrashing. With his body weight shifted forward, the beast's head was pinned to the ground, keeping its mouth pressed firmly shut. An alligator could close its jaws with tremendous force, but once its mouth was closed, it was relatively easy to keep it that way.

Bones worked his left hand forward to the tip of its snout, grabbed hold, and squeezed. Next, he worked his right arm free and slid it up to cover the beast's eyes. Finally, he pulled up on the snout until its neck was bent at nearly a ninety-degree angle.

Soon, the gator stopped fighting. Bones breathed a sigh of relief but held on.

"Nice job," said the red-haired woman. "What happens now?"

"We put something over its head until it calms down."

"And then what?"

"Then I let it go of it and hope for the best."

Her eyes went wide. "Are you kidding me? What if it comes right at me?"

"It shouldn't. Now, do you have anything I can use to cover its eyes?"

"Look at me. I'm stuck in the mud. And before you ask, no, I don't have a blindfold in my fanny pack."

Bones nodded. "It'll have to be your tank top, then."

The woman smirked. "Nice try."

"I'm not kidding. I'd use my own shirt but in order to take it off, I'd have to let go of this guy. Is that what you want?"

She tensed, fists clenched, but then the fight seemed to go out of her. "Fine. But if you ogle me, I'll punch you in the throat."

"Before or after we get you out of the mud?"

She flashed an angry scowl, then pulled her muddy tank top over her head. She wore a sports bra, which covered more than a swimsuit. Still, he got a nice glimpse of a flat stomach and smooth, fair skin.

"I told you, no ogling!" She flung the shirt at him. It struck him full in the face.

He ignored her. Still holding its jaws shut with one hand, he draped the shirt over its eyes, then spoke to it in soothing tones until it calmed down.

"Moment of truth?" the woman asked, her voice tight with anxiety.

"You got a name?"

"Mackenzie. You can call me Mack."

"All right, Mack. Here's the deal. When I jump off, the gator should turn and snap at me. If it's a typical gator, it's lost interest in dinner by now and will leave us alone, but just to be safe, I need you to be ready for me to pull you free."

"I've been ready since the moment I got stuck, genius."

Bones shook his head. "If I try and pull you out like you are now, the mud will work against us, and I don't know how solid the ground around you is. I need you to lie back like you're floating on water. That way, I can pull you free."

Mack quirked an eyebrow. "You want me to lie down in front of an alligator?"

"Do you really think you'll be better off standing knee-deep in the mud?"

She considered for a second, then let out a curse. "Fine. You win." Slowly, and with lots of swearing, she lay back in the gooey earth.

Bones looked down at the gator. It seemed calm, but who could say what it would do when he let it go? "Moment of truth," he whispered. He readied himself to move. As he let go, he sprang back, simultaneously pushing the gator forward. It didn't move far, but it bought him a few extra inches so that when the creature turned and snapped at him, its jaws closed on empty air.

"Come on, don't be like that," he said, slowly backing away in hopes of leading it away from Mack.

It worked. The gator advanced on him a few steps, let out a hiss, then turned and headed away. Bones didn't relax until it slid into a deep pool and sank from sight in the distance.

"Get me out of here before that thing comes back," Mack said.

"You didn't say the magic word."

"Please?"

Bones shook his head. "The magic word is 'beer,' and you're buying."

"Deal." She held out her hands for Bones to take hold. He pulled her free and helped her to her feet.

Mack looked him up and down, appraising him. "Not bad considering you're not Seminole."

"Don't believe that stereotype," he said. "But I'm impressed that you can tell us apart."

"You're Bones Bonebrake, right?"

Bones was surprised and suspicious in equal measure. "Who do you work for?"

"Myself, thanks to you." She glared at him.

"What's that supposed to mean?

She clenched her fists, but the fire suddenly went out of her. "Look, I've had a bad day. How about I buy you that beer and we start over? I think you'll be interested in what I have to say." She glanced down at her mud-caked body. "After I've showered of course."

"I will on one condition. You let me wash your back."

Mack shook her head. "I appreciate the help you gave me. Don't ruin it."

3

Key West, Florida

Captain Tony's was one of Bones' favorite dives. It was dark and musty with low ceilings. The building had originally been constructed as a combination icehouse and morgue. Though it was often crowded, Bones felt the good beer and live music made it worthwhile. He also found that the chaotic atmosphere made it the perfect place to hold a conversation when you didn't want to be overheard.

As they approached the bar, Mack looked around and frowned. "Interesting décor. I can see why you chose this place."

"You mean the cash?" Bones asked innocently. The ceiling and portions of the walls were plastered with layers upon layers of dollar bills on which customers had scribbled notes, probably enough to send a kid to college. "Or did you mean the license plates?"

"No, the other things."

"Oh, you mean the bras." Hanging signed and dated brassieres on the walls was another Captain Tony's tradition. "You should add one to the collection. It's a great place to leave your mark."

"Why would I want to do that?"

"Are you kidding? This is a historic bar! It was the original Sloppy Joes. Hemingway drank here! Jimmy Buffett drinks here. And it's haunted."

"Very impressive," she said dryly.

"Check this out." Bones pointed to a stool on which the name SEAN CONNERY was inscribed. "The second-best

James Bond drank here." Mack didn't take the bait. "Ted Kennedy has a stool here. So does Eric Clapton."

"I would have said those in a different order," Mack said.

Bones grinned and pointed to a tree growing up through the middle of the bar. "They used to hang pirates from there."

"And now they hang bras." She rolled her eyes to show what she thought of the décor.

"I give up," Bones said. "The Venn diagram of you and people who know how to relax would be a big circle and a tiny dot nowhere near it."

"Sorry," Mack said. "It is an interesting place. Ordinarily, I'd enjoy it, but this hasn't been an ordinary day. No offense, but I don't think I'm a fan of Florida."

"Florida is America's basement. It's damp, moldy, and full of bugs," he said, quoting a line from one of his favorite television shows.

Mack flashed a sly grin. "Alligators are dinosaurs, Bonebrake. You know that?"

"I see what you did there. You might be okay, after all. Let's grab a drink and you can clear away this cloud of mystery."

Mack ordered Pirate Punch, Bones a Dos Equis, and they settled into a table in the corner.

So, what were you doing out in the swamp, anyway?" Mack asked.

"Checking out the Lost City of the Everglades." He did not miss her flinch when at the words *Lost City*. "What did I say?"

"Nothing," she said. "I was just surprised. I've never heard of it."

"It's not a lost city in the ancient world sense. It's much more recent than that. Al Capone made moonshine there. Civil War soldiers encamped at the site."

"And what's your interest in it?"

"I was following up on a theory that Capone hid something there. Turned out to be nothing."

Mack laughed. "Okay, Geraldo Rivera. Don't you know what happens when you search for Al Capone's vault?"

"I do now. How did you know where to look for me, anyway?"

"When I couldn't track you down at home or at your boat, I paid a visit to Dane Maddock."

"I'm surprised he answered the door. He's… busy right now."

"It wasn't him. It was a blonde. Quite pretty, extremely rude. She wanted to know if I was somebody named Isla." She raised her eyebrows, questioning.

Bones nodded. Isla Mulheron had twice betrayed them. The last time, she'd also stolen something of great value from Maddock and Bones. "It's the red hair," he said as if that explained everything.

"Anyhow, she told me where to find you and closed the door before I could say thanks." She took a drink of her Pirate Punch and nodded in satisfaction. "You like searching for lost cities?" she asked with exaggerated casualness.

"I do," Bones said, pleased they were getting to the point at last.

Mack nodded. "Here's the deal. I'm a journalist. I persuaded my employer to send me to Cabras to follow up on… certain happenings."

Bones nodded and took a drink. He knew exactly which events she was referring to.

"Obviously, the story sounded farfetched at best, but my sources were reliable. I put my career on the line."

"Let me guess," Bones said. "When you got there, you found nothing."

Mack flared up immediately. She slammed her glass down on the table, sloshing punch over her hand. "You knew?"

Bones shook his head. "No, but I've learned to expect cover-ups in situations like that one."

"You've been in similar situations?"

Bones shrugged. If Mack thought Cabras had been farfetched, she'd never believe some of the things he and Maddock had survived.

"You don't have to tell me," Mack said. Nico Russo assures me you're the real deal. Plus, I did a background check on you."

"That photo of me in a John Deere hat is a fake by my friend Corey."

Mack smiled. "I'm sorry I didn't find that. Actually, I didn't find much of anything, and I'm very good."

"What can I say? I've led a boring life."

"Don't try to bullshit me. Somebody's sanitized your record, as well as that of Dane Maddock, Willis Sanders, Matt Barnaby, and Corey Dean."

"You *have* done your research," Bones said, impressed. Willis, Matt, and Corey were his and Maddock's crewmates.

Mack inclined her head, obviously pleased by the compliment. "You don't know the half of it. I got kicked out of Crazy Charlie's Casino in North Carolina just for asking questions about you."

"It's my uncle's joint. We stick together."

"I noticed. After that experience, I decided against reaching out to your sister. She seems the combative sort, no pun intended."

"Wise choice. She loves to kick people in the face." His sister Angel was a professional MMA fighter who was now pursuing a career in acting.

"I did, however, score a meeting with Grizzly Grant."

Bones winced. Don "Grizzly" Grant was a television presenter who specialized in adventure programming. He'd been blessed with a big heart, a bigger mouth, and questionable judgment.

"He says you found the Loch Ness Monster," Mack

said.

"You can't believe half of what Grizzly says. He's a Hollywood guy. Thinks he's Indiana Jones."

"Actually, he says your friend Maddock is Indiana Jones."

Bones sat up straight. "If he called me Short Round, I will smack the taste out of his mouth."

"He said you're more like the guy from the Mummy movies. Somebody O'Connell... You know, Brendan Fraser's character. Personally, I think Brendan is cuter than you."

"I think this is the first time in history a Cherokee has been compared to a Jewish guy playing an Irish-American character, but I'll take it."

Mack flashed a shy smile. For once, there seemed to be genuine mirth there. Then she grew serious. "I don't expect you to spill your guts to me. But Grizzly showed me what you guys found in California. You're the real deal, and I need you."

Bones gave a single nod and waited for an explanation.

Mack took out a tablet and called up a satellite photograph showing dense jungle terrain. She slid it across the small table to Bones.

"What am I supposed to be looking at?" But his trained eye spotted it immediately. Glimpses of straight lines and right angles among the dense tangle of green. "Ruins. Where is this place?"

"Deep in the heart of the Congo."

"Why would anyone bother to take satellite photographs of that part of the world? There's nothing there."

She glanced away, a guilty expression on her face. "A contact of mine who works in federal law enforcement recently took part in a raid on a suspected dealer in black market antiquities, and he found what he believes to be a journal belonging to Henry Morton Stanley.

Bones perked up. Stanley was a legendary journalist and explorer best known for his travels in central Africa and his search for David Livingston. He was credited with uttering the iconic line, "Doctor Livingston, I presume?"

"In reviewing the journal, he came across an account of Stanley's discovery of what he called, "A lost city teeming with riches.""

"Never heard that story," Bones said.

"Apparently, Stanley kept it a secret because he planned to return someday. That day never came."

Bones nodded. Even today, a trek into the depths of the Congo River basin was difficult, expensive, and perilous. "Where do you come in?"

"Law enforcement has no interest in the contents of the journal. But my friend recognized it as being right up my alley. He also knew that I'm down on my luck after Cabras. So, he passed the information along to me. I pieced together the clues and pinpointed the general location."

"How did you get the satellite photo?"

"Another contact. We had a… fling a while back." Her cheeks turned red and she took a drink.

"No judgment here. I like flings."

"Anyway, there is very little satellite coverage of this area, but he did find this one photo right where I said it would be." She didn't quite keep the note of triumph out of her voice.

Bones stared at the photo. European explorers were renowned for "spotting" lost cities and treasure troves in remote locations, yet few of them actually proved to be true. Of course, he and Maddock knew from experience that not all such reports were false. And in this case, it seemed that Stanley had, in fact, found a ruin in a location where such construction was virtually unheard of.

"It seems like there really is a lost city. Do we have any idea if there really was a treasure there?"

"Stanley doesn't say, but I did find something

interesting. Shortly after he died, his grave was dug up. The authorities kept it quiet, which wasn't hard to do in 1904. It's not as if a story could go viral back then." She shrugged and went on. "The culprit was caught after he tried to sell the ring and pocket watch he stole off of Stanley's corpse. When they searched his home, they also found a piece of a stele which they determined to be of African origin, and a gold nugget larger than a man's fist. The Congo is known for its gold production."

"And they believe these items were buried with Stanley?"

"Where else would a petty criminal at that time and place have gotten his hands on such artifacts?"

Bones tugged absently at his ponytail, thinking hard. "Any idea what happened to them?"

"The gold was returned to his family, but the fragment of stele ended up in the Royal Museum of Central Africa, donated by his son Denzil, along with hundreds of other items."

"Tell me you have a contact there."

Mack smiled. "I do now. I visited there, made a friend who located it for me. It's such a small piece and there seems to be nothing special about it, so it hasn't been on display in decades." She reached over and swiped the screen.

The photo showed a flat piece of gray stone. On it was a carving of a stylized gorilla. The style was unfamiliar, and Bones said so.

"I haven't found anything like it," she said. "I think it might be the product of an isolated group of people."

"This is one of the remotest and deadliest places in the world and there's probably no treasure. You know that, right?"

"The city itself would be enough to get my career back on track. I'll pay you well, regardless of whether or not we find any treasure. Not that the authorities are likely to let us keep it."

Bones thought it over. It was dangerous, to be sure, but he'd been through much worse. Besides, if there was ever a cure for boredom, this would be it.

"All right, I'm in." They shook on it and then toasted to a successful mission. "By the way, does this city have a name?"

"Stanley called it Mbanza Mpimpá. It's a Kikongo term"

"What's that in English?" Bones asked.

Mack's expression was unreadable as she replied.

"It means City of Night."

4

Bones scooped up a handful of river water and poured it down the back of his neck. He closed his eyes and tried to ignore the heat as the leaky motorboat chugged along the sluggish tributary of the Congo River. With each bob of the small craft, the old boat took on more water. He closed his eyes and tried to tune out the sputtering of the engine.

"Is our transportation not up to your standards?" Mack asked. She could be prickly at the best of times but the farther they got from civilization, the grumpier she became.

"It's cool," Bones said. He didn't mind a leaky boat. What he didn't like was limping along the Congo River without so much as a paddle…or an ice-cold beer to wet his whistle. All he had on board was lukewarm bottled water, as well as dry rations and their equipment. They were a hell of a long way from the modern world.

"Mr. *Bone*," said their hired guide, a man who could barely understand English. "You will help?" He looked down at the two inches of water in the bottom of the boat and made a scooping motion with his free hand. The other was busy piloting the boat.

"Sure thing. I'd rather not sink before we get where we're going." He began bailing water with his cupped hands. Mack didn't offer to help. He didn't comment either. He was the hired help and she was footing the bill. And it was something to do.

He kept scooping until the remote village of Kitoko appeared around the bend. Mack had told him that Kitoko was a Kitongo word that meant "beauty" or "loveliness," but the only thing lovely about it as far as Bones could see was the rickety dock that meant he could finally get the hell out of this boat.

After they docked and unloaded their gear, Mack paid the river guide and promised him double when he returned in ten days' time. They estimated that would be time enough to reach the city, make a thorough photographic record, and return to the village.

The man's eyes went wide as she placed the money in his palm. He smiled, bowed deeply, and said, "Matondo!" *Thank you!*

They grabbed up their gear and looked around. As it were, Bones and Mack were the only two people within earshot. The only other living thing near them was a rail-thin dog. It looked up at them from its half-eaten fish and cocked its head to the side before returning its attention to its meal. The place was eerily quiet. Just a few huts, and no villagers in sight. Bones instinctively reached for the Glock he wore holstered at his hip.

"What are you doing?" Mack asked, looking around for danger.

"Just getting ready in case a zombie staggers out of one of these huts."

Mack almost grinned. "It does have an apocalyptic feel to it, doesn't it?"

Just then, an elderly man peered out from one of the huts. His eyes fell on the two newcomers and he flashed a gap-toothed grin.

"Welcome," he said in heavily accented English. "American?"

"I am," Bones said. "A true American, that is. The white is descended from immigrants." Bones winked.

The wizened old fellow bobbed his head and grinned as if he understood.

Mack rolled her eyes. "Why can't you at least try to make

a good first impression?"

"My good looks take care of that for me." He smiled. "Besides, Red, annoying you makes me happier about being here."

"I hate you almost as much as I hate being called Red." Mack's pressed her hands to her temples.

Just then, a tiny woman with dark skin and snow-white hair emerged from the same hut. She scolded the old man rapidly in one of the several languages common to the region, then turned to the two visitors.

"Why are you here?" She spoke with the confidence of someone who was accustomed to having her questions answered promptly. And although she was barely five feet tall, Bones felt as if she were somehow looking down her nose at them.

"I don't suppose there's a bar in this town," he joked. "Somewhere I could get a hippo burger medium-rare?"

The little woman stared at him until his smile melted. Then she turned to Mack.

"Are you from the American government? We want no trouble."

"You've had people from the government here?" Mack asked.

The old lady just stood there nodding staring. She wasn't going to offer a reply.

Mack hurried on. "We are looking for Pepsy."

The woman nodded. Then, she turned and disappeared behind a row of locals who had begun to gather. All of them carried a weapon of some sort—clubs, knives, and one incredibly old shotgun. None of them spoke.

"I don't get it," Bones said. "I jokingly ask for a beer and I'm a jerk, but you ask for a Pepsi and it's all good?"

"Pepsy is a common man's name in this part of the world," she explained.

Just then the old woman returned with a young man. He was tall and skinny. His arms and legs were too long for his body, his head a touch overlarge. His eyes were white circles against his dark skin.

"I am Pepsy," he said simply. "What do you want?"

"Good to meet you," Bones said. "I'm a big fan of your cousin, Coke. But only mixed with Jack Daniels."

"I do not know these people," Pepsy said flatly.

Mack flashed Bones an angry look, then politely held out her hand. "Hello, Pepsy, my name is Mackenzie Moore. This," she tipped her chin at Bones, "is Bones."

Pepsy grinned. "Bone?" His eyebrows scrunched, lost in deep thought. "Funny name. Don't let dog chew on you." He pointed to the skinny mutt lying in the sun nearby and laughed.

Bones' mouth hung open, unable to formulate a proper response. The corner of Mack's mouth twitched. She was clearly holding back a smile, thinking the turnaround on Bones was hilarious.

Pepsy thought that Bones' name was the odd one at the table? It wasn't the first time Bones had gotten a sideways glance from someone, questioning his name. This, however, took the cake.

"We are conducting research and we want to hire you as a guide. Doctor Fetisov should have told you about us."

Pepsy bit his lip. His eyes fell.

"What's the problem?" Bones asked, knowing that look.

"Igor," Pepsy replied quietly, leaning in closer to them. "Gone missing."

"Explain." Bones wasn't messing around. If someone went missing, particularly someone they needed in order to get their job done, then he wanted to know everything he could and help any way he could.

"Went upriver." Pepsy looked over his shoulder, obviously nervous. He lowered his voice. "Igor and two men never come back. Weeks ago."

"We are headed upriver as well," Mack said. "If you'll take us, maybe we will find him along the way."

Pepsy shook his head. "Too dangerous."

"I'll pay you double your normal fee," Mack said. Still, the man did not relent. "Do you at least have a boat we can rent?'

"Money can't buy much out here," Bones said. "You need to offer him something he can't find anywhere else."

"I'm not sleeping with him," Mack said softly.

"That's not what I'm talking about." Bones dug into his pack and pulled out a deck of playing cards he'd picked up on his last trip to Vegas. Each displayed a different naked woman. "Here you go, Doctor Pepper, check this out."

Pepsy smiled and his eyes grew wide. He reached out to take the cards, but Bones pulled them back.

"Not until you take us upriver." He pocketed the cards. "And there are some good ones in here, let me tell you. And you're definitely going to want to see the Jokers. The girls are all…"

"That's enough." Mack looked from Bones to the still-smiling Pepsy. "Even in the jungle, men are pigs."

"What's it going to be?" Bones asked.

Pepsy cupped his chin and narrowed his eyes. But before he could answer, a commotion came from the other side of the village. The young man turned and dashed away. Several of the others followed at a jog. They returned a few minutes later.

Pepsy's entire demeanor had changed. He appeared frantic. He spoke rapidly to the little old woman. Her expression did not change—she was obviously an extraordinarily strong person, but Bones saw her knees wobble for just a second.

"What's going on?" Bones asked.

"Rebels take Lisy, my sister."

Bones grimaced. Among the perils of this region were pockets of rebels, or "freedom fighters" as they preferred to be called. Some stood in genuine opposition to the government, while others used it as an excuse to prey on the weak.

"When did this happen?" he demanded.

"Not long. You help find her?" He eyed the Glock at Bones' waist. "You help us, I guide you anywhere in jungle."

Even if they hadn't needed the man's help, Bones would not have left an innocent woman suffer the depredations the rebels surely had in store for her.

"How many are there and how are they armed?"

Pepsy translated for Bones and the villagers. "Three. One rifle, two…" He searched for the word, then settled for miming a pistol with his thumb and forefinger like a child at play.

"I can handle it," he said.

"We go, too," Pepsy said.

"And me," Mack added.

"I need people who can move quickly and silently through the jungle." He turned and glared at Mack. "They also have to obey orders immediately and without question."

Mack stared at him for a full three seconds before begrudgingly agreeing. "I don't let my ego get in the way of good sense. You're the SEAL so you're in command."

Pepsy cocked his head in the same way the dog had when they'd entered the village. "Seal?" He pressed his forearms to his sides and slapped his hands together as if they were flippers.

"Never mind that," Bones said. "We need to move fast. Come on."

5

To Bones' relief, Pepsy and the two men he had deputized moved skillfully in the jungle. They moved fast, but still managed to choose their steps with care so that they made no sound. Mack wasn't quite as accomplished, but she kept up with the group and made little noise. Except for the time a forest cobra slithered across their path, and she had to cover her mouth to suppress her tiny yelp. Bones couldn't entirely blame her for that one.

It was easy to follow the trail the kidnappers had left behind. They were on foot and making no effort to hide their tracks. They probably believed they had nothing to fear from the villagers. But they hadn't counted on someone with Bones' skill set.

"Four sets of prints," Pepsy said. "She is still alive."

"We want to keep her that way," Bones said. "So be careful with that shotgun," he added to the sole armed villager. Pepsy translated and the man nodded.

It wasn't long before they heard voices. Men barked what sounded like sharp commands and a woman's voice snapped back angrily. Pepsy grinned at the sound.

"Lisy can be, how Americans say it?" He scratched his head. "Woman dog?"

Bones saw the look in Mack's eyes and decided against answering. Instead, he lowered his voice to a whisper.

"If it comes to a fight, what will your sister do?"

"Strong but not fool. She will fight unless no hope."

Bones shook his head. "If you tell her to run, do you think she will?"

Pepsy shrugged. "I will try."

They closed in on their quarry and stalked them until

the rebels and their hostage came to a halt. Lisy's wrists were bound in front of her. One of the men shoved her roughly to the ground and barked an order. Another produced a water bottle and offered it to her. She replied with what sounded like a curse word. The man chuckled and said something to his companions, who also laughed. The men sat down and passed around the water bottle. They seemed confident that no one was following them. Perfect!

As Bones hurried back to the group, he formulated a plan, and with Pepsy's assistance, he quickly gave everyone their assignments. Mack looked as though she wanted to debate some of the finer points, but she held her tongue.

Bones crept back to his hiding place, drew his Glock, and took aim at the man carrying the rifle. He waited until he heard the whistle that told him his companions were in position.

Bones squeezed the trigger and his shot found its mark, taking the man in the chest close to the heart. The surviving men sprang to their feet. Behind them, on the side opposite Bones, a shotgun blast rang out, followed by shouts. Bones took aim and a second man fell, just as Pepsy began calling out for his sister.

Unfortunately, Lisy was every bit the fighter her brother had said she was. She lurched to her feet and took a wild swing at the last rebel. He ducked and punched her in the jaw. She stumbled back into Bones' line of fire.

"Move!" Bones growled, trying to get a clear shot.

Pepsy continued to call out until Lisy abandoned the fight and ran off in the direction of her brother's voice with the rebel hot on her heels.

Bones took off after him. He was a crack shot, although Maddock claimed to be better. But even with Bones' skill, he doubted he could hit a moving target in the jungle while he was also running. Hopefully, his contingency plan would work.

Lisy continued running toward the sound of Pepsy's

voice, which was growing louder. They broke into a clearing and Bones finally caught clear sight of the rebel. The man had caught up with Lisy.

Just as he reached out to grab her, Mack stepped out from behind a tree. She wielded a thick branch like a baseball bat. The man barely had time to react before she swung.

And Mack hit a homer with that swing. She caught the rebel on the chin and knocked him clean off his feet. He went down flat on his back. His breath left him in a rush, and he lay gazing glassy-eyed at the sky.

"Nice swing, Red," Bones said.

"Not my first rodeo," she said, glaring at the fallen man. "I've met a lot of guys in my life who needed to be hit with a stick."

"They are animals," Lisy said. She was an attractive woman, with big eyes and full lips, but her expression was hard, her tone harsh. "They would have done terrible things to me." Her English was much better than Pepsy's.

The dazed man on the ground caught his breath and began to babble.

"What's he saying?" Bones asked.

Pepsy frowned. "Sacrifice needed."

"A sacrifice?" Bones asked. "Who were they planning to sacrifice her to?"

Pepsy barked a harsh question. Bones didn't need an interpreter to understand his reply.

"Mokele-mbembe."

"I know that name," Mack said. "Isn't it something to do with folklore, children's stories?"

Before Bones could reply, they heard footsteps approaching Bones raised his Glock but lowered it when he saw it was the three villagers who had joined them. When they saw Lisy, they hurried over to greet her.

"I'll ask again," Mack said. "What is Mokele-mbembe?"

"It's a legendary cryptid," Bones said. "The name means

'one who stops the flow of rivers.'" Bones turned to Pepsy. "Ask him where they were planning on taking her."

Pepsy asked and the man replied with a single word.

"Upriver," Pepsy translated.

"Where, exactly? Can he be more specific?"

To Bones' utter astonishment, before Pepsy could ask the question, Lisy snatched the long-bladed knife that her brother carried and plunged it into the prisoner's heart.

"What the hell did you do that for?" Bones demanded. If the Mokele-mbembe were real, this man might have offered a clue where to find it.

"Mokele-mbembe is evil," she hissed. "Stay away."

Bones let out a deep sigh as he watched the last of the kidnappers expire before his eyes.

"Fine," he said, then turned to Pepsy. "You're taking us upriver just like you promised."

Pepsy grimaced, looked as if he were going to reply, but then he nodded.

"I keep word. We leave tomorrow?"

Bones shook his head. "I'm not giving your sister a chance to talk you out of it. We leave immediately."

6

Pepsy's motorboat was every bit as leaky as the one that had brought them to Kitoko. Bones and Mack passed the time bailing water and discussing the legend of the Mokele-mbembe.

"According to legend, Mokele-mbembe is a water-dwelling creature, part elephant, part dragon, that lives somewhere deep in the Congo River basin," Bones explained. "She is huge, with a long, flexible neck and a muscular tail it uses as a weapon. Some call her a hippo killer."

Mack raised her eyebrows in surprise. "It would take something like a dinosaur to kill a hippo."

That was true. Contrary to the popular image of the hippo as a lazy, slow-moving creature, the hippo was a powerful beast, highly territorial and aggressive. Its size and thick hide made it a deadly enemy, particularly in the water, where it could move quite well.

"From the description, it sounds like a brontosaurus," Mack continued.

"Something like that, but smaller," Bones said. "Some called it a forest-dwelling sea serpent."

"I knew you were into cryptids, but I didn't realize you were an expert."

Bones shrugged. "I've picked up a few things here and there. When I was a kid, I read every book I could find on cryptids, unsolved mysteries, conspiracy theories. And I've watched a metric crapton of those sorts of shows and documentaries."

Mack's lips puckered as if she'd sucked on a lemon. "Tell me you're not one of those guys who goes out into the woods and beats on trees to try and communicate with Bigfoot."

"I haven't been on a Bigfoot hunt, yet." Bones said. The Florida Skunk Ape was not the same as Bigfoot, and therefore didn't count. "Maybe I will someday."

"You're a true believer, then?" she asked, her tone neutral.

"I wouldn't say that, but I'm always open to new evidence when it comes to cryptids."

Mack sat up a little straighter and brushed a stray lock of red hair out of her face. "Was Grizzly telling the truth about Nessie?"

"Grizzly is a good man, but he's also a Hollywood guy. He loves to spin a good yarn, no matter how thin the thread."

"That's not an answer," she said.

"Correction; it's not the answer you wanted." Bones began bailing water while Mack settled into a discontented silence.

"How about you, Pepsy?" she finally asked. "What can you tell me about Mokele-mbembe. Do you believe in it?"

"I do not understand," Pepsy said over the coughing and sputtering of the engine.

"Do you believe it is real or not?"

Pepsy cocked his head and his brow furrowed. Finally, he shrugged. "My English poor."

"You just don't want to answer the question. You're as bad as he is," Mack said, firing up.

"It's the way you asked the question," Bones said. "To him, the Mokele-mbembe is as real as any other creature that lives in the Congo. To ask him if he believes in it would be like me asking if you believe in your dog."

"I don't have a dog," she muttered. She folded her arms and stamped her foot, splashing water on both of them.

"There are better ways to bail," Bones said. He didn't mind. The lukewarm water felt good on his face.

"What's the matter? Afraid of a little water?" She scooped up a double handful and flung it at him. Bones ducked out of the way. Pepsy didn't move fast enough and caught a faceful.

"Please, Miss Red," he protested. "I never see Mokele-mbembe. I know what Mister Bone knows."

"It's Bones. Plural."

"Or you could call him by his real name, Uriah," Mack said.

Bones splashed her in the face. "I hate that name."

"I heard that about you." Mack wiped her face with her shirttail, giving him a tantalizing glimpse of a creamy flesh over taut abs. Pepsy made a soft "hmm" of admiration. Quickly she lowered her shirt and cast an angry glare in his direction. "Keep your eyes on the river," she said.

"Sorry, Miss Red," he replied.

"Did he tell you to call me that?" she demanded. Neither man replied.

They lapsed into silence until Bones grew bored with bailing.

"I'm surprised you didn't come across the Mokele-mbembe legend while you were researching the lost city." Behind him, Pepsy let out a grunt of surprise. Bones kicked himself for that slip of the tongue. He expected a tongue-lashing from Mack, but instead, she glanced away.

"I might have seen the name, but it wouldn't have been something I'd need to know. If I saw it, it didn't stick in my memory."

Bones had a feeling there was more to it than that, but he kept his thoughts to himself. They were on a dangerous expedition and it wouldn't do to have friction between them. At the moment, they were getting along reasonably well.

"Is there any solid evidence for Mokele-mbembe?" she asked. "Photographs, casts of tracks?"

"Only a lot of eyewitness accounts, as far as I know,"

Bones said.

"Any other legends of living dinosaurs around here?" Mack asked.

"Roy Mackal, the famous Nessie investigator, conducted two expeditions searching for Mokele-mbembe. He didn't find any solid evidence, but he did collect stories of other dinosaurs."

"What kind?"

Bones scratched his head. He had done a bit of reading on the subject in preparation for their trip into the Congo. Not that he expected to find a living dinosaur, but it never hurt to be prepared.

"There was one that was sort of like a cross between a Triceratops and a rhino."

"Emela-Ntouka," Pepsy offered.

"That's the one. And there was another which was more like a Stegosaurus. Had plates along its back." He put his hands behind his neck to illustrate."

"Mbielu-Mbielu-Mbielu," Pepsy said.

Bones laughed. "The dino so nice they had to name it thrice."

Mack rolled her eyes. "What about predators? Should I expect a T-Rex to come stomping out of the jungle?" Her voice was all forced casualness, but Bones could tell she had something on her mind. He couldn't blame her for being afraid. In this place, the everyday dangers were more than enough to put the most experienced explorer on high alert.

And with that thought in his mind, he spotted something up ahead that froze his marrow. Dark shapes moved near the riverbank. Huge humps in a line like the humps o a sea monster, sliced through the water, headed in their direction.

"Hippos!" Bones warned

Pepsy let out what sounded to Bones like a curse and turned the craft toward the shore.

"I always found them cute and funny," Mack said, her

voice tight, "but they're actually pretty scary."

"You're damn right," Bones said as the hippos closed in on them. The river suddenly seemed impossibly wide, the boat painfully slow.

"Can you go any faster?" Bones said.

"I can if you get out, big man," Pepsy said.

"Could you shoot them?" Mack asked, glancing down at the Glock Bones wore on his hip.

"Sure, if you want to piss them off even more," Bones said. "I'd need a weapon with a lot more stopping power than this handgun to have any chance of slowing one down, and even then, it's dicey."

The hippos closed in. They appeared to grow larger with each passing second. The riverbank seemed hopelessly far away. Bones considered what he knew of hippos. Hippos couldn't swim. Instead, they moved by pushing off objects or the riverbed itself, relying on their buoyancy to help them glide through the water.

"Do something," Mack said. Her tone was one of annoyance rather than fear or concern, as if Bones were failing to do his job.

Bones drew his Glock, took aim, and fired a warning shot into the water a meter from the lead hippo. As he had expected, it had no effect.

"Try again," Mack said.

"Waste of bullets." He looked to the shore, considered the boat's rate of speed, and then looked at the hippos. There was an outside chance they would make it to shore, but it was going to be close. Every second was going to count. He stuck his Glock into his rucksack, which was secured in the middle of the boat. His boots followed.

"What are you doing?" Mack asked.

"Swimming for it. Pepsy was right. Without my weight, you'll stand a better chance of making it to shore."

"And what about you?"

Bones flashed a grin "Don't worry about me. I'll meet

you on the shore." Before he could change his mind, he stood and dove into the water.

After a day spent baking under the sun, the sudden plunge into the river felt like being immersed in an ice bath. It energized him and he kicked hard and began to swim for all he was worth. It was a calculated gamble. With the hippos bearing down on the boat, perhaps they wouldn't notice him before he made it to land, and without his two hundred plus pounds to carry, hopefully the boat would reach the riverbank safely.

The plan appeared to be working. He swam toward the shore unmolested. Meanwhile, Pepsy's boat had gained a measure of speed. But still, the hippos closed in.

"Hey!" he shouted at the beasts. "Over here!" He began to tread water. "Come and get me!"

"What are you doing?" Mack called out.

"Trying to distract them!"

It almost worked. One of the hippos veered off course and headed to intercept Bones. The rest continued after the boat.

"Dammit!" He swam again, pouring all his reserves of strength into the effort. As a former SEAL and a marine archaeologist, Bones had spent much of his adult life on or in the water, and he was an excellent swimmer. But outpacing a hippo was virtually impossible. The average hippo could move two to three times faster than an Olympic swimmer, and Bones was no Michael Phelps.

The hippo that was pursuing him sank beneath the water, but the v-shaped ripple on the surface of the water told him the creature was still bearing down on him. He swam harder, fighting the current that steadily carried him back downstream.

Upriver, Pepsy's boat had nearly made it to shore. And then Mack shouted something. With a thump and a splash, the boat was thrown upward. Mack and Pepsy went hurtling through the air. As she flew, Mack let out a string of curses. The two landed hard on the muddy riverbank.

Get out of there! Bones thought.

As if they had heard his thoughts, the pair struggled to their feet and dashed for the cover of the jungle. But the hippos didn't follow. They slammed into the boat a couple more times, then turned away.

Now there was only one hippo to be accounted for—the one coming after Bones. It was now so close that Bones could see the dark shape closing in. He remembered the story of a woman who had escaped a hippo by punching it in the eye repeatedly, but not until she had been badly mauled. But right now, his options were limited.

Still swimming, he reached for his Recon knife. But he was too slow. The hippo shot up, caught him on top of its snout, and tossed him into the air.

"Holy crap!" Bones shouted. He landed flat on his back in the shallow water. His breath left him in a rush. He rolled over and tried to get to his feet. His hands and knees sank into the muck of the riverbed, holding him down. The hippo closed in.

Bones drew his knife and readied himself to make a last stand, but the hippo veered away, satisfied that this intruder had been put in his place. Relieved, Bones drew in a ragged breath and shouted at the retreating beast.

"That's right! Walk away while you still can!"

"You really kicked his ass." Mack was walking along the bank, smiling at him. "I definitely hired the right man for the job."

"We all made it safely to shore, didn't we?" Bones said, sheathing his knife and slogging through the shallow water.

"That's true. The boat wasn't so lucky. It's got a huge hole right up at the front."

"The bow," Bones said automatically.

"Right. Anyway, it won't float again. Pepsy is beside himself."

"We'll buy him another one." Bones hated to be so

coarse, but what else could they do? Right now, they were all truly up the creek.

7

Bones was relieved to discover that their gear and provisions were still secure inside Pepsy's ruined boat. Their guide had gone from enraged to despondent. When they assured him they would replace his boat and double his compensation, he managed only a brief, crooked smile.

They hid the boat at the jungle's edge and headed upriver. According to Pepsy, the village that was their destination was not far away.

When they arrived, a voice called out from above. A young man armed with a bow and arrow peered down at them from the upper branches of a tree. He and Pepsy engaged in a rapid-fire conversation. Bones caught the name Igor Fetisov, but he understood nothing else. Finally, the young man's tone softened, and he waved them on to the village.

They were greeted by a group of nervous-looking villagers. A tall, slender woman with big, brown eyes, greeted them in broken English. Pepsy introduced their party.

"I Izefia. You look for Russian?" she asked.

"Yes, Doctor Igor Fetisov," Mack said. "Have you seen him?"

She shook her head. "Long time."

The young man standing guard atop the stockade shouted something down to her.

"Juma saw Russian." She paused, narrowed her eyes. "Four days." She held up four fingers. "My English bad."

"You've got me beat. I can't speak any other language as well as you speak English," Bones said.

She frowned, then a smile spread across her face.

"Thank you. You Mister Bone?"

"Close enough," Bones sighed.

"Some people call him Uriah," Mack chimed in.

"Screw you, Red," Bones replied automatically. He looked up. "Yo, Juma. Which direction was he headed?"

Juma got the gist of the question without the help of translation. He pointed west.

"Do you know where he was going?" Mack asked.

Once again, Juma understood. He gave a long reply which Izefia translated within the limits of her English vocabulary.

"Found new gorillas." She paused, shook her head. "Gorillas live alone. Juma not know where."

"Understood," Bones said. He was slightly disappointed to learn that "new" gorillas didn't mean an undiscovered species. Still, he was grateful for the lead, even if it were a thin strand.

The villagers invited them to stay the night, and they gratefully accepted. It was late in the day and twilight was upon them. They stowed their belongings in an empty hut, then joined their hosts for a meal of roasted meat and vegetables. Bones wasn't too particular about where his protein came from, but he chose not to ask.

Izuma approached him with a sly expression on her face. Her hands were hidden behind her back. Bones cocked his head to the side and frowned.

"You like?"

For a moment, Bones thought she was asking if he liked her, which he did. Then she showed him what was hidden behind her back. A can of beer. The label read Primus. Bones had enjoyed one upon their arrival in Kinshasa. He had learned that it was by far the most popular beer in the Democratic Republic of the Congo. But to find one out here seemed nothing short of a miracle.

Bones threw back his head and laughed. "Like it? I love it! Where did you get this?"

"Man leave here."

That was good enough for Bones. He accepted the beer from her with profuse thanks. "How about you and I split this?"

Izuma frowned. "Split?" She made a chopping motion.

"He means share," Mack said. To illustrate, she snatched the beer from Bones' hand, popped the top, took a swig, then passed it to Pepsy. The guide hesitated, then laughed and took a drink.

"That was not cool," Bones said, grabbing the can from Pepsy.

"Not cold. Sorry," Izuma said.

Before Bones could clarify, an old man barked Izuma's name. Her eyes went wide, and she hurried away.

"I think you should steer clear of her," Mack said. "She's nice enough, but the men of the village don't appear to like the attention you're paying to her.

Bones grinned. "Jealous?"

"Hardly. I just don't want you to get us killed."

"Fair point." He took a swig of beer. It tasted slightly sweet and finished with a hint of bitterness. Not bad for a mass-produced brew. "You never told me why you're looking for this Russian. I take it he's a primatologist?"

"He's trained as a herpetologist."

"What's he doing studying gorillas?"

Mack didn't quite meet his eye. "He has a variety of interests."

"Like what? Mokele-mbembe?" Bones joked.

"He's interested in any sort of animal, really." Even in the firelight, Bones cold see her cheeks turning red.

"What are you holding back?" When she didn't reply, Bones pressed. "Look, we're out in the middle of nowhere and we need to rely on one another, and that includes trust. There's something you aren't telling me."

"I'm not hiding anything important to our expedition. It's just that Doctor Fetisov is sort of a controversial figure.

Rather than engage with him on an academic level, his peers dismiss him as an eccentric who has strayed off the traditional path and over the deep end."

Bones froze with the can of beer an inch from his lips. Slowly, he lowered it.

"Are you talking about the White Russian?" The White Russian was a name that appeared from time to time on the cryptid message boards, usually in connection with legends of surviving dinosaurs and primitive hominids.

"That name is a pejorative," Mack said.

"Chill. I think you know that I'm open-minded about this sort of stuff," Bones said.

The tension seemed to flow out of Mack. "That's what I figured. It's just that my colleagues at Nat Geo would react very differently. I've worked hard to be taken seriously in my profession, and after Cabras…"

"I promise to hear you out with no judgment. Drink on it?" Bones took a drink then passed the beer to her. She took a swig and passed it on to Pepsy. "Spill it."

"Igor Fetisov was once a highly respected herpetologist in Russia. Over time, he became more open-minded about possible undiscovered species. Little by little, he lost credibility with his peers." Her expression grew dark and she grabbed the beer from Pepsy and took a swig.

"I can understand that," Bones said.

"He eventually landed in the Congo Basin, where he has lived for five years."

Bones nodded. It made sense that a man who was passionate about undiscovered species would find a home in one of the remotest places in the world.

"I did a deep dive into some of the more obscure online cryptid communities," Mack continued. "I found a few mentions of Fetisov coming across a ruined city. It was set in a valley, sheltered by a dense canopy of trees. He said that where beams of sunlight filtered through the trees, the ground shone gold."

"You think he found Mbanza Mpimpá." Bones suddenly understood. "It's because of the gorilla stele, isn't it? Maybe one of these isolated great ape populations lives near the lost city?"

She fixed him with an amused smile.

"Dammit, stop grinning at me." He crossed his arms. "The only time a chick is allowed to look at me like that is after a couple of hours on a Serta Perfect Sleeper."

Her face turned up. "First of all, gross! Second, yes, I think it's perfectly reasonable to assume the builders of Mbanza Mpimpá carved images of the animals they saw around them."

"Are you sure you're not thinking about the Michael Crichton novel? You know, the super-smart, evil apes?" Her withering stare wiped the grin off his face. "Just trying to lighten the mood." Finding someone who had been to the city would be a tremendous help. Knowing the GPS coordinates was one thing. Knowing how to get there was another thing entirely. And then a new thought struck him. "I'm curious. If the ground shines gold, why would they call it the City of Night?"

Mack had no answer.

8

The following day, Juma guided them to the place he had last seen Igor Fetisov. Pepsy joined them, vowing to repay his debt to them for rescuing his sister. Bones suspected the man was reluctant to hoof it all the way home. The pair searched the ground until Bones found partial boot prints. When he announced his discovery, Mack raised her eyebrows and gave a nod of approval. Coming from her, it felt like a round of the "Hallelujah Chorus."

They followed the trail for hours, finding just enough signs to keep them moving. At midday, they took a break for a light meal. Mack and Bones had packed protein bars, and Pepsy rounded out their lunch with a pear-like fruit he called moabi.

Refreshed, they set out again. It wasn't long until Bones spotted movement in the jungle up ahead. He raised his hand in warning. No telling what was up ahead.

They crept forward on silent feet. Listening hard, Bones heard a scuffling sound, saw a flash of gray and white. *Don't let it be a grumpy silverback.* His concerns were allayed moments later when the figure up ahead let out a curse. In Russian.

"Gav-no!"

Bones had spent just enough time in Russia and around Russians to understand a few choice words, most of them inappropriate for polite company. He called out the first thing that came to mind.

"Blyat!" Bones shouted.

The figure up ahead stopped moving, fell silent.

"What did you say?" Mack whispered.

"He said 'shit' and I said 'whore.'"

Mack glanced at him, one eyebrow raised. "Why would you say that?"

Bones shrugged. "I don't know a lot of Russian."

"But you just happen to know that word?" she said.

"It's not by accident. Everywhere I go, I make it a point to learn three words: beer, bathroom, and prostitute."

"I can't tell if you're joking or not," Mack said.

"Where is prostitute?" Pepsy whispered. Mack balled her fist and shook it at the guide, who held up his hands in a defensive gesture. "Sorry, Miss Red."

"Stop calling me that." Mack stood and called to the man up ahead. "Doctor Fetisov, is that you?"

"I am Igor. Who are you?" the man called back.

"My name is Mackenzie Moore. We'd like to talk with you."

"Come on, then."

They emerged into a tiny clearing where a lean-to had been constructed in front of a small fire pit. A slightly disheveled looking man sat hunched beneath the shelter's slanted roof.

Igor Fetisov was a man of about fifty. He was solidly built, with a full head of gray hair and a stubbly mustache and beard. When he saw them, he raised a hand in greeting.

"It is good to see you, Pepsy. Who are your friends?"

Pepsy introduced his companions.

"What's up, Doc?" Bones said, earning an eye roll from Mack.

Igor laughed. "I love Bugs Bunny! They don't make good cartoons anymore. Not that I own a television." His belly laugh turned into a wheezing cough. He waved them over to join him. They took seats on the ground.

"It is unusual to meet anyone out here, especially Americans," he said.

Mack was about to speak, but Bones gave a tiny shake of his head. She was a cut-t0-the-chase, time is money type. Bones had some experience dealing with people like Igor.

Cryptozoologists often became worn down by the constant stream of ridicule. Consequently, they tended to become prickly whenever a stranger brought up any topic related to the unknown.

"Mackenzie is a reporter for National Geographic," he said. It wasn't true today, but it had been until recently.

Igor scratched his chin thoughtfully, then nodded. "I thought the name sounded familiar. I have read some of your articles. You are very good." Mack beamed at the compliment. "Are you on assignment?"

"Freelance," Mack said.

"We understand you have been studying gorillas," Bones said.

Igor nodded slowly. "What is your interest in the gorillas?"

Mack quickly understood Bones' strategy. Ease into the subject. "With all the problems in the world, it's easy for people to forget the plight of the great apes. But people have grown weary of all the stories about poaching. I want to give them something hopeful, something to capture their interest. A story about isolated gorilla populations that are thriving beyond the reach of modern humankind."

"What led you to me? My work is not exactly well-known these days."

"The story needs more than gorillas." She was so smooth that Bones almost believed she had rehearsed her pitch. "We need something else to capture the readers' interest."

Igor frowned. "Such as?"

"An archaeological find, like an undiscovered city."

Igor stiffened. "I am afraid you have the wrong person. I study animals."

Mack took her time opening her pack and taking out a sheaf of papers protected by a double-layer of sturdy Ziploc bags. She withdrew the satellite image of the lost city and handed it to him. Igor took a long look at it.

"This does not look familiar."

Mack took out another photo—the stele. "How about this?"

As soon as his eyes fell on the photo Igor sprang to his feet. "I will not help you."

"Please, Doctor Fetisov," Mack said. Bones was surprised the word 'please' was part of her vocabulary. "It is very important."

"Do you know what will happen when this place is found? It will no longer be a secret. The city will be looted, and the gorillas slaughtered."

"And that is why my article is so important." She held up a satellite photo and shook it at him "This photograph was taken by a US military satellite. They know about the city. There are already rumors on the internet. Someone is going to find it sooner or later, and it will probably be the worst sorts of characters. Let's get out in front of the story, generate public awareness and support. It can't be hidden forever so let's find a way to protect it."

Igor looked as if he wanted to believe her. "Even the most ethical among the government here will want the city for the gold."

Bones sat up a little straighter. So, there was gold in Mbanza Mpimpá!

"You're right," Mack said. "The government will take every ounce of gold. But who cares about that? We want to protect the gorillas and the city itself. Our goal is to convince the government that Mbanza Mpimpá has value even after the gold has been taken away. Imagine the fees they can demand from archaeologists, primatologists, other scientists."

"Scientists," Igor said with a note of derision. He sat back down, his head hanging. "I want to believe what you say, but what makes you so certain people will be interested in an old ruin?"

"No one cares about an old ruin," Mack said, "but a lost city of gold? *That* truly is gold."

Bones nodded. The woman could sell milk to a cow.

"You cannot imagine how dangerous it is there," Igor said. "I have been observing other gorilla troops of late. I haven't felt safe returning to the city. I hope the gorillas are safe."

"I know what it's like to know the truth but have to keep your mouth shut because people are so obtuse that they won't even look at your evidence." Bones said. "We have military confirmation of the site's existence. We have an award-winning journalist." He looked at Mack. "You have won awards, right?

"Oh yeah," she replied, nervously chuckling. "Tons."

Bones nodded. "She's associated with one of the most prestigious publications in the world. And for whatever it's worth, you've got a highly decorated Navy SEAL attached to the project." He saw a spark in Igor's eyes. Time to set the hook. "We're going to put you in the news for all the right reasons. You'll be the man who discovered Stanley's lost city, the guy who protected one of the world's last untouched gorilla populations. Nat Geo will make you the freaking centerfold." Igor chuckled at that. "And you can take a copy of the magazine to every one of your critics, and tell them to roll it up real tight and stick it in their…"

"I take your point," Igor said with a rueful laugh. "The two of you make quite the team. But there is something I must know. Do you genuinely believe in my work, or do you only want me as a guide?"

Bones leaned in a little closer and locked eyes with the man. "What would you say if I told you satyrs are real and they are mean as hell? And I can't tell anybody about it."

Mack leaned over and whispered in his ear. "What is this about satyrs?" Bones didn't reply. The corner of his mouth twitched. Let her wonder.

Igor gaped at him. A slow grin spread across his face, then slowly melted as he read the sincerity in Bones' eyes. Finally, he gave a single nod.

"Very well. I will show you the way to the city, and you will help me give the scientific community and their closed way of thinking a well-deserved enema."

Bones shook Igor's hand.

"I think you and I are going to get along just fine."

9

They set off right away. Igor led them on a winding path through the dense jungle. He seemed to know every twist and turn. Bones was grateful for his presence. The going would have been much slower had they been forced to find their way on their own.

The farther they went, the quieter the jungle became. Some might find it eerie, but Bones saw a calming beauty in an environment like this, except for the times when something was, in fact, trying to kill him. Something that seemed to happen all too often.

The trees were lush. They seemed to stretch on forever, but Bones knew it couldn't last. The Congo Basin's jungle was shrinking daily due to deforestation. But, unlike other parts of the world, where corporate interests were largely responsible for the destruction of rainforests, deforestation in this region was primarily a consequence of subsistence agriculture.

War and political instability had driven people to the brink of starvation. Now, families used hand tools to carve small farms out of the jungle. They would work the plot until the nutrients in the soil were depleted and then move on to another plot of land. This so-called "shifting agriculture" and other small-scale clearing was responsible for most of the deforestation. Of course, that wouldn't last, either. Mack was right, finding Mbanza Mpimpá and rallying support behind its preservation constituted the best chance for the city and the local gorilla population to survive.

Still, the rainforest was massive in size, and few outsiders had explored it. Maybe, if things in the region calmed down, the incursions into the jungle would diminish.

"I came this way originally," Igor explained. "Myself and two assistants."

"What happened to them? Bones asked.

"The life here was too hard for them." He glanced down at the ground.

"How long to the city?" Mack asked.

"We can be there in two days if all goes well."

"That's it?" Mack asked. "I thought our destination would be more remote than that?"

Igor smiled. "Two days *is* remote out here, Ms. Moore. You could be a half a day's walk from some form of civilization and never know it."

They came to a deep ravine. A fallen tree, smooth with age, spanned its depths. Crossing it was child's play for Bones. He easily made his way across, though it gave a little bit beneath his weight. He didn't like that at all. The others were lighter than him and had an even easier time of it.

They had gone only a short distance when Mack pointed at a fallen tree that blocked the path. The tree was large and looked like it had been there for some time. Different types of vines and other stringy plants had grown all over it, securing it further. There were a few more trees down on the other side too, adding to the natural blockade.

"What's the big deal?"

"That tree looks like it was ripped from the ground. See?"

She was right. Something had torn it down. The exposed roots indicated that this was not a tree that had rotted and fallen over.

"Strong wind?" Bones suggested halfheartedly.

"Why is it only this tree that looks like that?

"Gorillas sometimes pull trees from the ground," Pepsy said, not looking at the fallen tree.

"That would be a big-ass gorilla," Bones said. No one had anything to add.

Mack seemed to be perfectly comfortable out in the wild. She paused periodically to snap photos or jot down notes, moving with a confidence bordering on recklessness. Bones recognized the same tendencies in himself, but in another, it caused him consternation. He preferred to be the risk-taker and let someone else watch his back.

"You move well out here," he said, hoping that if he acknowledged her skills, she would feel less of an urge to demonstrate them all the freaking time.

"Can we not talk about the way I move?" she said, squinting at something up ahead.

"I'm talking about the way you move in the jungle. I'm glad I'm not stuck with a total greenhorn."

A smile flickered at the corners of her mouth, but it turned into a frown. "You seem surprised. Why? Because I'm a woman?" One hand went to the machete she wore on her hip.

"No, because you're white."

That stopped her in her tracks. While she tried to figure out whether he was joking, Bones kept walking. She caught up with him a few seconds later.

"You think you're funny, don't you?"

Bones pretended to give the question serious consideration. "Yeah, pretty much."

"Well, let me tell you…" She stopped dead in her tracks and seized him around the forearm. She pointed at something up ahead. "What could do that?"

He followed her extended finger.

A tree, healthy with a thick trunk, had been snapped off at about the level of Bones' head. It appeared to be fresh, too. Sap oozed down its trunk. Once again, none of the other trees had been touched.

Instinctively, they looked around, as if whatever had done it but they saw and heard nothing. As they moved closer, Bones spotted something embedded in the trunk of the tree just below the break.

Mack rushed ahead and let out a gasp at what she saw.

"What is it?" Bones said.

"It's a scale, reptilian. And it's huge!

She was right. It was a thick, pebbled scale, olive green, roughly rhomboidal in shape. And it was almost the size of Bones' hand!

They moved in to give the scale a closer inspection. It resembled the skin of a crocodile in some respects, but there were subtle differences in the mottling, the shape, and of course, the size.

Mack locked eyes with him. "You don't think it could be…"

Bones did think it could be, but he didn't want to be the first one to say it. He took a few steps back and inspected the area around the tree, looking for signs of the creature that had left this bit of its armor behind.

The area around the tree had been trampled, low-growing vegetation flattened, fallen limbs crushed, but could find no prints. The layers of detritus were too dense, the soil here firm and rocky.

"I'm going to search a little farther out," Bones said. "This thing must have left a trail."

"There is no need!" Igor said.

Bones turned to see that both the Russian and Pepsy were hanging back. Igor was a herpetologist and a cryptid nut. He ought to have been the first one checking out the scale.

"You already know what this is, don't you?" Bones said.

Igor nodded.

"Mokele-mbembe?" Mack asked.

"Yes."

"Holy freaking crap," Bones muttered. "Another secret you were trying to keep."

"It has not been easy," Igor admitted. "As the forest shrinks, animals are driven deeper into it. Which sometimes disturbs the current residents."

"Mokele-mbembe is real! Finally, something good happens to me!" Mack began taking photographs of the site. First some closeups of the scale, and then some wide shots. Next, she passed the camera over to Bones so that he could get a few shots of her beside the scale. Bones decided not to tell her she had a spider crawling up her arm. Unfortunately, Mack wasn't bothered. She held out her arm and mugged for the camera.

When she was finished, Igor drew a large specimen bag from his pack along with a pair of tweezers. With practiced patience and a steady hand, he plucked the six-inch-long chunk of scale from the log and stowed it away.

"I want to follow its trail," Mack said.

"Me, too!" Bones added.

Igor shook his head. "It is far too dangerous. Mokele-mbembe makes the angriest hippo seem a gracious host."

"I need to document its existence," Mack said. "Ultimately this is for its own protection."

"You said I was to take you to Mbanza Mpimpá. Not on a dinosaur hunt."

"This all part of the same effort," she said. "Please. This single scale," she pointed to the bag Igor held, "is magnificent, but you know it won't be enough for the so-called authorities."

Igor considered this for a moment. "Mokele-mbembe's preferred range runs along one of the smaller branches of the Congo River. If we follow the river on our way home we will pass through its territory. I will take you there after we have gone to the lost city. That is if we survive."

10

It was nearly dark when Igor called the group to a halt. He explained that up ahead lay a village where they would ask to bed down for the night.

"The people here are very suspicious of outsiders," he said. "They know me. Wait here and I will go talk to them. I will come for you when they say it is all right."

"We have tents. We can just camp here."

Igor blanched. "I would not spend the night out here unless I had no other choice."

Bones wanted to ask if wooden huts really afforded that much protection, but the Russian was already traipsing off into the jungle.

"That was weird," Mack said.

Igor returned shortly and guided them to the village. When they finally arrived, Bones did a double-take. The village was surrounded by a wooden stockade. He shook his head. A heavy double-gate barred their way. Here he was, in the middle of the Congo, and he was approaching the closest thing to a Jurassic Park gate as he had ever seen. He could almost hear the movie score playing in his mind.

"Why would they need something like that?" Mack asked.

"Many dangers," Pepsy said.

She quirked an eyebrow. "Like the Mokele-mbembe?"

Pepsy didn't reply.

A legendary dinosaur and a King Kong-sized wall. Bones pressed his fingers to his temples and rubbed.

"Just freaking wonderful," he sighed. "What the hell have I gotten myself into?"

The residents of this small village barely looked at Bones

bad Mack. They ushered the pair to one of the small huts that were common to small villages in the Congo river system. Mack looked as if her eyes would pop out of her head when she realized they were bunking together, but the tension that seemed to ooze from the locals stayed her tongue. Their hosts provided them with food—fish and some sort of tuber vegetable, both of which Bones skewered and roasted kebab style over a small cookfire.

Mack sat across from him, looking through her notes, mumbling to herself. She would occasionally jot down something new, her eyebrows creasing inward as she did. Mack would also bite her lip while she wrote, looking quite cute whenever she did it. If she wore pigtails and overalls, Mack would look like your prototypical country tomboy. The light freckling on her face added to the imagery. There weren't many of them, but the tiny, sprinkles of color seemed to be precisely applied to the right spots. A couple on her cheeks. A few on her nose. One on her chin.

Pepsy was off somewhere, and like Igor, he was chatting it up with the local populace. The villagers were uncomfortable around the Americans, but hopefully, if they had any important details to share about the lost city or about Mokele-mbembe, they would open up to the Russian or the Congolese man.

"What is your impression of Doctor Fetisov?" Mack bit her lip and waited for his reply.

Bones scratched his chin. "That's tough to say. He comes across as a little bit off, but that's not unusual for someone who lives his life so far removed from civilization."

Bones passed her a skewer of steaming fish and veggies. Mack accepted it with a nod and a little sound that might have been a word of thanks. Bones decided to take it that way.

The fish had a strong flavor, the tubers were tough, and with no seasoning, the meal was bland but filling. When they were finished, Bones stretched out on the soft earth and lay, hands behind his head, fingers laced together, gazing up at a sliver of starry sky that peeked through the foliage.

"What do you think he's so afraid of in Mbanza Mpimpá?" Mack asked quietly.

"Considering how many things out here can kill you, no telling."

"That's my point. He seems particularly frightened of going there."

"True, but he agreed, so whatever it is, he must believe he can survive it. And if he can, so can we." He looked over at Mack and winked.

Mack bit her lip once more but nodded.

Then, a chorus of loud cries rang out.

What the hell?

Bones and Mack looked at one another before darting out of the hut. Neither one of them were taking any chances. Bones still had his Glock and Mack wielded a machete. She also brought her camera, which hung from a strap around her neck and bounced around as she ran.

A grinding sound caught his attention. It came from his left, further down the main road, toward the wall. He looked just in time to see a section of the wooden stockade burst, exploding towards him in a shower of wooden shrapnel. There, emerging from the destruction, and in all its horrible glory, was their monster!

Mokele-mbembe was very much what Bones had always imagined. She was about the size of a large bull elephant, if that elephant had a long, serpentine neck and a muscular tail like an alligator. A large African elephant stood about four meters tall at the shoulder and had a body about five and a half meters long—roughly twelve feet by sixteen feet. Mokele-mbembe matched that with ease. While she resembled a Brontosaurus in general shape and appearance, her neck and tail were shorter in proportion to her body. Bones put her at about forty feet long from nose to tail. And boy, was she mad.

The beast opened its hideous mouth slightly, resonating a sound like grinding stone. Its hiss was what Bones and Mack heard earlier, just before it obliterated the gate and parts of the wall.

"Well," Bones said, "that's not terrifying or anything."

"Now we know for sure why they built a wall around this place, as if there was much doubt."

Even as dangerous as the current situation was, Bones' mind was working through every conceivable scenario. What was she? A new species? An offshoot of Brontosaurus. How did she move with such agility? Did that mean she was not primarily a water dwelling creature as most believed? And more importantly, what could they really do against this thing? Arrows pinged off her tough hide. A bullet wouldn't do much better. Besides, even if he had an elephant gun at hand, Bones wouldn't shoot this thing except in the last defense of his life. It was a surviving species of dinosaur. Its very existence was miraculous!

The villagers continued to attack the angry dinosaur. Flaming arrows traced lines of gold through the night sky and sent up sparks as they deflected off her hard scales. Each salvo only seemed to raise her ire.

Bones thought he could see how this story would play out. Smash, roar in anger, smash, roar in anger…and so on.

He backed away slowly, pulling Mack along. "We need to leave."

"But—"

"No buts, Red," Bones interrupted, getting her attention with the nickname she hated. "This," he held up his Glock, "is going to do jack squat to that." He pointed at the creature. "See how they're mostly aiming at the head even though it's almost impossible to hit? Their only hope is to annoy her until she goes away."

"Fine, but I'm getting some photos first." She raised the camera, focused, and began clicking.

Mokele-mbembe froze. Her head whipped around. She was staring right at them. Suddenly, she didn't look like the big, dumb dinosaur on the Flintstones.

"Oh, damn…"

Bones and Mack froze in place, but Bones had a feeling it wouldn't matter how good or bad the thing's eyesight was. Reptiles had a highly developed sense of smell, and this one was no exception, flicking its long, black tongue in and out of its mouth, tasting the air.

With a sudden fury, Mokele-mbembe made her move, launching her weight against the stockade wall. It sagged backward, the logs snapping with loud pops and cracks until it sounded like the Fourth of July in a redneck neighborhood. They watched in horror as she backed up and charged again. The wooden wall still held, but it wouldn't withstand another charge.

"Move!" he shouted, shoving Mack aside. Together, they ran back to their hut. "We'll grab our gear and find a place to hide." They ducked inside the hut. Bones grabbed his pack and slung it over his shoulder. "Ready?"

"Are you kidding me?" Mack had already made herself at home, and her possessions were scattered everywhere.

"I'd hate to see what you'd do to a hotel room," Bones said.

"I promise you will never share a room with me." She continued stuffing items into her pack until she finally announced she was ready to go. No sooner had she made the proclamation than a sound like thunder came rolling toward the hut. There was a loud hiss that sound like it was right on top of them.

"Down!" Bones grabbed Mack around the waist and bore her to the ground like a football tackle moments before the little hut was annihilated by something huge. Bones opened one eye to see an olive-green blur shred the structure as if it were made of toothpicks. Mokele-mbembe's tail passed over them by mere feet.

"Holy shit!" Mack yelled as splinters, leaves, and broken branches rained down on them.

"Quiet!" Bones hissed. He braced himself for another attack, but the dinosaur let out another hiss and thundered away.

They could hear Igor above them yelling, shouting in fright. He was somewhere close by, but it was impossible to see him while blanketed by the thick layer of jungle remnants.

"We need to help him!" Mack said.

"How?"' Bones asked.

"I don't know. Figure it out. Aren't you supposed to be Indiana Jones?"

"Not according to Grizzly," Bones said with a touch of resentment.

"You can be Lara Croft for all I care. We've got to do something."

"Fine," he said. "But you stay here."

"Buried under this crap?"

"It will hide you from sight and maybe cover your scent a little bit." He sniffed the air. "Your breath smells like fish, by the way."

Mack rolled her eyes. "Oh, do shut it. Now, go save the day."

Bones grimaced and began to crawl out from under the rubble. He had no idea what he was going to do.

11

The village had gone crazy. The locals were running in every direction. A few still tried to fight the rampaging dinosaur. Others tried to distract her with torches. Most simply ran. Bones calmly cracked his neck, then took off after the beast, which lumbered in the direction of Igor's hut.

Igor had been given a Swiss Family Robinson-style tree hut. It was apparently reserved for honored guests. Bones could hear him crying out in fear.

"Hang in there, Igor," Bones whispered as he sprinted toward the hut.

Something like a small explosion erupted overhead and debris rained down. Mokele-mbembe had smashed the wooden staircase that led up to the hut. Igor's angry shouts turned to shrieks. The dinosaur drove its head against Igor's hut, again and again, punching gaping holes in its flimsy walls. Her powerful tail whipped back and forth, keeping the villagers at bay.

Igor's head poked out of the door, and he froze when he saw the staircase was gone. He hesitated, then took something from around his neck and tossed it down to Bones.

Bones caught it and frowned. It was a whistle carved from bone. It was roughly shaped like the Mokele-mbembe, and its surface engraved with a variety of symbols. He could tell in an instant it was ancient.

"She will follow the whistle!" Igor shouted. "Blow it!"

Bones pressed his lips to the hollow tail and blew a puff of air through it. It made no sound that he could hear, but the effect on the angry dinosaur was immediate. She froze, and her head slowly turned in Bones' direction.

"Oh, hell no." He took off at a dead sprint, heading for the gaping hole in the stockade wall. Behind him he heard the creature let out another hiss. More sounds of shattering wood, more screams from Igor. The dinosaur hadn't given up. Barely able to believe what he was doing, Bones blew the whistle again.

This time it worked. Glancing over his shoulder, he saw Mokele-mbembe turn away from the huts and take off after him. Bones reached the gaping hole in the wall and leaped through. An important rules of surviving a wild animal attack was always give the animal a way out. If an animal felt penned in, it would certainly lash out.

He made a sharp right turn and sprinted around the village wall. Behind him, Mokele-mbembe was in hot pursuit. She thundered through the gaping hole in the wall, sniffed the air, then turned and chased after him.

Bones quickly picked up the faint trail they had followed to the village. Right now, he had only one idea, and he'd need luck on his side for it to work. Only his excellent night vision and a lifetime of experience in forest terrain prevented Bones from becoming ensnared in one of the jungle's many traps. He leaped over fallen logs, ducked beneath low-hanging limbs, and slipped between close-growing trees. These same obstacles, which Bones skirted easily, were an annoyance to the angry dinosaur. She smashed through the low limbs, bounced off the trees, and even stumbled once over a particularly large fallen log. At least, Bones thought he saw her stumble. But still, she kept coming.

"Why haven't you given up yet?" he huffed. Bones was in excellent physical condition, but he was tired from the day's travels and he finally feeling the burn. His legs were beginning to tire, and he was no longer breathing easily. This had to end soon.

"One last card to play."

Up ahead, the steep ravine barred their way. As fast and agile as she was, there was no way Mokele-mbembe was going to leap across that gap. If only Bones could make it to the other side.

The dinosaur's thundering feet sounded as if it were right on top of him. She had nearly caught up. Still, Bones had to slow his pace. To run full sprint out onto the slippery log bridge would be suicide. Quickly running out of good ideas, or ideas of any kind, Bones drew his Glock as reached the edge of the ravine. He fired two shots in rapid succession. The first missed but the second caught the creature in the neck. As expected, it did no visible damage. Still, it did the trick. Whether it was the sudden flash of light, the explosion of sound, or a measure of pain from the slug striking its hide, Bones couldn't say, but Mokele-mbembe flinched. She turned her head and closed her eyes for an instant, enough to make her collide with the thick trunk of an iroko tree.

Mokele-mbembe let out a guttural roar and reeled to the side. She staggered toward the edge of the ravine.

"Come on!" Bone whispered. He was only a few steps out onto the log, but he was frozen in place, unable to look away as the enraged dinosaur finally recognized the danger and put on the brakes. Six tons of Jurassic death skidded toward the sheer drop-off. Her huge feet dug trenches in the soft earth. Closer!

And then Mokele-mbembe did something unexpected. Something downright clever. She wrapped her long tail around a nearby tree and used it to slow herself. The force nearly uprooted the tree, but it did the trick.

"Holy freaking crap." Bones said, stunned.

Mokele-mbembe locked eyes with him and let out another hiss. Bones could swear she smiled at him.

"See you!" Bones turned and ran. Even with his sharp eyes, the jungle-filtered starlight provided scant illumination. He was running little better than blind.

Mokele-mbembe hissed again, seemingly just over his shoulder. He glanced back to see a watermelon-sized, serpentine head coming right at him!

The world slowed down around him. He was suddenly hyperaware of all his senses. He felt the spongy log give a little as he stepped down, saw a single star reflected in one of its oily black eyes, smelled its rancid breath.

See you, world! It's been real!

He turned his head and closed his eyes. The creature's jaws clacked as they snapped closed. Pain burst in the back of his head.

Damn! That hurt! Am I dead?

And then he realized he was still running. He put his hand to the back of his head but felt no injury there. But there was a lot less hair.

"You got a chunk of my ponytail, you bitch!" And then he laughed. He was beyond the reach of Mokele-mbembe's serpentine neck!

He looked back and could just make out the outline of the massive beast. She wasn't going away.

"Why don't you just give up?" Bones grumbled as he continued to move across the log. There was a gap in the jungle canopy above the ravine, which allowed just enough starlight through that the log appeared like a light gray smudge beneath his feet. He decided to keep his foot in the center.

That worked for three steps before his boot nearly skidded off the side. He needed more light.

Light!

"Idiot!" He smacked himself in the forehead. Mokele-mbembe let out another hiss. He glared at her. "Not you."

In his flight, he had forgotten his omnipresent Mini Maglite. He rarely opted for it in situations like this, preferring to rely on his own night vision. But it was not often that he found himself in a spot like this. He took out the small flashlight, switched the beam to red, and turned it on.

After the almost total darkness, even the filtered light seemed like the light of day. Bones blinked away an afterimage and began moving again. He was beyond the halfway point. Nearly there.

And then the log began to tremble beneath his feet. He turned and shone his light behind him. Mokele-mbembe stood with its foot upraised. Bones understood in an instant.

"You are such a…"

And then the dinosaur brought its foot down onto the log with all her might. Bones felt the force of the blow through his legs and all the way up his spine. Heard the soft wood begin to splinter. Felt the log give way.

He jumped.

12

Mack pushed her way out from underneath the rubble of the collapsed hut. She brushed aside a big green frond of some tree she couldn't name and peered out into the firelit night. Villagers carrying torches ran past her. In the distance, a flaming arrow had set a hut alight.

She looked around. There was no sign of Mokele-mbembe. Maybe Bonebrake really had managed to scare it off. Relieved, she stood, brushed herself off, and took a moment to retie her ponytail before heading in the direction of Igor's hut. It was time to find the rest of her party.

No one paid her any mind as she strode through the village. Already they were hard at work putting out fires and repairing the gaping hole the rampaging dinosaur had smashed in the stockade wall.

Mack's journalistic instincts kicked in. Her camera still hung from a strap around her neck. She raised it, took a deep breath to steady her shaking hands, and began snapping photographs. It wasn't fear that caused Mack's extremities to twitch, it was the massive amount of adrenaline that had been dumped into her system as a result of the prehistoric conflict. She didn't lower the camera again until she reached Igor' hut.

"Oh my God. Igor!"

Igor's tree hut lay in a mangled heap on the ground. Mokele-mbembe had torn it apart. Pepsy stood gazing down at the ruins. Blood streamed down his cheek from a shallow cut. She hurried over to him.

"Are you all right?" she asked, hurrying over. "Where is Igor?"

Pepsy merely pointed down at the pile of wood, leaves, and rope that had been the tree hut. A battered hiking boot attached to a thick, white leg stuck out.

"Dammit," she said, jaw clenched. Igor was supposed to guide them to Mbanza Mpimpá. He was also a decent guy, she supposed. "What about Bonebrake?"

"He led Mokele-mbembe out into the jungle," Pepsy said voice low.

Mack snapped her attention to the local. "He did what? That moron!" No one could be that brave, so clearly, Bonebrake was an idiot. "Should we go after him?"

Pepsy frowned. "Mister Bone saved my sister's life. I would help him if I could. I do not think we can."

Mack nodded reluctantly. He was right. They couldn't kill the dinosaur, or even harm it apparently. Bonebrake had done the only sensible thing and drawn it away from the others. Still, it seemed wrong to stay here and do nothing. "Let's get Igor out from under here," she said briskly. "He deserves a decent burial."

They set to work, delicately removing the debris that covered the fallen scientist. When they finally uncovered his body, he didn't have a scratch on him. Only the blood flowing from one ear indicated that he'd suffered a fatal injury.

As they lifted his body clear of the fallen hut and laid it on the ground, Mack noticed something tucked inside his shirt. Something hard and rectangular. Pepsy was looking the other direction and she quickly reached inside the dead man's shirt and grabbed it. It was a journal, and it must be important for Igor to tuck it inside his shirt in the middle of a dinosaur attack.

She opened it and flipped through. It was not a scientific journal, but a personal one. Most entries were written in Igor's own pidgin dialect—mostly English with a generous helping of Russian, sprinkled with a bit of French and what Mack presumed were native words and phrases. Some passages began as fully English, then flowed into pure Russian, and back to English again.

She came to a series of maps that covered several pages. They had obviously been updated and revised over time. The lines and words had been written with different pens, and some were old and smudged. This would take some time to decipher. She wondered if Bonebrake could help, then laughed at the thought. When it came to myths, monsters, and mayhem, the man knew his stuff, but he was no scholar.

At the thought of Bonebrake, she looked around, wondering if he would ever return.

"I am sure Mister Bone is safe," Pepsy said, accurately reading the expression on her face.

Mack nodded. She hoped he was correct. Without Bonebrake, she wondered if they would get out of this alive.

Bones leaped into the air as the log bridge collapsed underneath him. All his senses were alive as he hurtled through dark nothingness. The dim beam of his flashlight slashed through the darkness as he flew.

Great job! You escaped the falling bridge by jumping off it into the deep ravine.

His light swept across the jungle-draped cliff on the far side of the ravine. An afromosia tree grew at the edge of the cliff; a curtain of vines dangled from its lowest branches. Bones reached out and caught a handful of jungle growth with his free hand.

Please hold, he thought as he swung forward. Above him, the loud crack of a branch snapping split the night. The vines gave way and he dropped a meter before his fall was arrested.

The cliff face was coming closer. The vines began to give way again. One by one, they snapped. Bones calculated the distance, the speed at which he was swinging, and the rate at which the vines were snapping. It was going to be close.

The veiled cliff came closer. His makeshift rope continued to fail him.

Bones let go.

His momentum carried him forward. Above him, he heard the limb that supported the vines crack just as he slammed into the cliff face. Bones scrambled for a handhold and managed to snag a protruding root. He held on tight and closed his eyes as the vine-laden limb fell.

A jagged corner of the limb caught his shoulder on the way down. Pain tore through him and he lost his grip on the root.

"Holy crap!" he shouted as he slid down the cliff face. His sweaty palms scrabbled for purchase and managed to grab hold of a small outcrop of rock. Thankfully, it supported his weight.

He hung there, catching his breath. His flashlight was long gone. Bones looked up and noticed that the moon was gone. Its illumination had been blotted out. Without it, he was essentially blind. His feet sought toeholds and found them. Slowly, carefully, feeling his way bit by bit, he began to ascend the cliff face.

Each time he reached out for something to grab onto, he prayed his hand didn't close on anything that would bite or sting. At long last, his hand found the ledge and he hauled himself over. The moon's light was present here too. He rolled onto his back and lay catching his breath and taking stock of his injuries. Best he could tell, his worst injury was a cut over his right shoulder blade where the falling limb had struck him. Otherwise, just the usual bumps, bruises, and scrapes. He hauled himself to his feet and saw, to his relief, Mokele-mbembe heading off to the south. She wasn't a predator and he wasn't the prey. She was merely a territorial creature—one who apparently hated the sound of the old bone whistle Igor had given him. His hand felt for the whistle underneath his shirt. It still hung there. He was relieved. Although he couldn't imagine ever wanting to use the thing again, it was a fascinating artifact and he couldn't wait to examine it. But for now, he had to skirt the ravine and make his way back to the village.

"This," he said to the trees, "really sucks."

It was well past midnight when Mack heard footsteps outside her tent. She grabbed her machete and quietly moved to the mesh window set in the door. In the dim light, she could just make out the silhouette of a tall, muscular man with a ponytail.

"Thank God," she whispered, then raised her voice a notch. "Bonebrake, get in here," she hissed, unzipping the tent door, and pulling back the flap to let him inside.

"Sharing a tent? I like it?" But there was no heart in his jest. She could hear the weariness in his voice.

"I hate to admit it, but I'm glad you're back."

"I almost didn't make it back," Bonebrake said, sitting down heavily. "And when I did, the villagers almost didn't let me back in."

Mack nodded. Since the attack, their hosts' attitude toward the interlopers had become borderline hostel. According to Pepsy, it was only the high value these people placed on hospitality, and a measure of gratitude to Bonebrake for leading the dinosaur way from the village, that kept the Congolese from turning their guests out in the middle of the night.

"Are you hurt?" Mack asked.

"Got a cut on my shoulder," he said. "I don't think it's too bad."

"Take your shirt off. I'll clean it up." Mack dug out her first aid kit, while Bonebrake removed his torn and bloody shirt. She flicked on her flashlight and winced at what she saw. Scars crisscrossed his tanned, muscular back. Some of them were faint, others more recent.

"Your back looks like a road map," she said, inspecting the laceration on his shoulder.

"And every street is a dead end," he said.

She tried to smile but it came out as a wince as she cleaned the cut on his back. He didn't even flinch as she rubbed ointment into the wound.

"It's not too bad," she said. "You've obviously dealt with worse." She bit her lip. "And speaking of worse, Igor screwed us over."

"What do you mean?" Bonebrake turned to face her.

She handed him the journal. "There's a lot in here I can't yet decipher, but I worked out his maps. He wasn't leading us to Mbanza Mpimpá. He intentionally led us in right into the heart of Mokele-mbembe's territory."

Bones let out a low curse as he flipped through the pages.

"To make matters worse, the villagers are blaming him for the attack."

"I think he did." Bones closed the journal, then removed the object he wore around his neck. It was some sort of bone amulet on an old leather cord. She hadn't noticed it before. He handed it to her.

"It kind of looks like a dinosaur." She realized it was hollowed out. "Is it some kind of whistle?" She raised it to her lips and Bonebrake immediately snatched it away.

"That's exactly what it is. When the Mokele-mbembe attacked his hut, Igor tossed this down to me and told me to use it to get her out of here. It's like a dog whistle to that thing."

Mack instinctively drew back, horrified at what she had almost done. "Igor must have used it to induce her to attack." She frowned. "But why wait until we were inside the stockade to do it? There was no guarantee she would break through the walls, and even if she did, it's not like he could point her at the two of us."

"I doubt he wanted to kill us. Scare the crap out of us, sure. Convince us to go home, absolutely."

Mack nodded, tapping her chin thoughtfully. "Why do you think he's so desperate to keep us away from the city?"

"I don't know," Bonebrake said. "But I'm going to find out."

13

They left the village early the following morning. No one invited them to stay for breakfast. Bones didn't blame them. Although the villagers had all survived the attack, several had been injured, and a great deal of damage done to their village. All because they had offered hospitality to outsiders.

They hurried off, eager to leave the village behind. Using Igor's notes, and with Pepsy's assistance, they had plotted a course to Mbanza Mpimpá. It wasn't far away, as the crow flies, but Pepsy warned the path would be difficult.

Bones now carried his own machete, along with his Glock and recon knife. He regretted the loss of his ever-present Maglite, but he found a small flashlight among Igor's belongings.

Better than nothing, he thought.

It wasn't long before they came across Mokele-mbembe's tracks.

"She went this way," Bones said, kneeling before more of the creature's tracks. "Toward the city."

"How do we know it's a she?" Mack asked, eyebrow raised.

Bones shrugged. "I didn't see any… equipment if you know what I mean. Plus, she was a fireball of hate from the get-go." He moved off before Mack could respond.

Bones and Mack had their personal packs with them while Pepsy carried their supplies, camping equipment included. He declined offers to distribute the burden more evenly among the three explorers. He now believed he owed Bones two life debts—one for rescuing his sister and another for leading the monster away the previous night.

"This reminds me of the *King Solomon's Mines* movie

from back in the eighties," he said, trying to lighten the mood. Igor's death was weighing heavily on all of them.

"I didn't see it," Mack said.

"It was just okay, but Sharon Stone was awesome!"

"Who is Sharon Stone?" Pepsy asked.

Bones groaned and rubbed his forehead. You know, *Basic Instinct*?"

Pepsy shook his head.

"Never mind," Bones said, "Forget I said anything."

"Shhh…"

Mack hushed him, and before he could retaliate, he understood why. The jungle around them was deathly silent, like before. Perhaps the creatures that called this part of the rainforest home had abandoned it when Mokele-mbembe came through. The trio quickly discovered that their path to the lost city roughly aligned with the dinosaur's trail.

"Must tell you something," Pepsy said, getting Bones and Mack's attention. They stopped and waited for him to continue. "Village elders say Mokele-mbembe not alone."

"You mean there are more of her kind?" Bones asked. He supposed there had to be a breeding population of some sort unless she was the last of her line.

Pepsy shook his head. "Other…" He frowned; his eyes turned toward the sky. "Different dinosaur."

Bones looked at Mack, who nodded.

"You don't seem surprised," Bones said. "What's the deal?"

"It didn't seem important at the time, or even believable. But another bit of information I got from my inside source—the one who provided the satellite image—was an account of a raid on a black-market antiquities dealer in the States. He had artifacts from this area, including the toe of something like a T-Rex."

"A fossil is hardly proof of another surviving breed of dinosaur."

Mack's cheeks went scarlet. "It wasn't a fossil. It still had tissue, preserved of course."

Bones stiffened. What else might she be hiding?

"Look, I'm sorry," Mack said. "I didn't take it seriously. Hell, I didn't even bother to research Mokele-mbembe. It didn't seem worthy of mention until we actually found her. Well, she found us. But we haven't seen any sign of another dinosaur, so maybe it's not even a true story."

"That's not the point," Bones said. "How am I supposed to trust you? What else don't I know?"

"That's everything! I swear." She looked him in the eye.

"All right, Red. But consider yourself on probation."

The trio hiked for several hours before settling down for the night. Thankfully, their way and that of Mokele-mbembe finally diverged. Bones was in no hurry to encounter the beast again.

He quickly announced that he would take first watch, letting the weary Pepsy and the emotionally drained Mack rest. Mack, like Bones, would never admit it, but she was badly shaken by fatigue and the events of the previous days.

While the other two retired to their tents, Bones reclined against a tree and reflected on recent events. They had gotten lucky back in the village. Only Igor had been killed, and since he called the creature down on them, it was sort of deserved.

He was an hour into his watch when he heard the sound. It was a loud, guttural sound, something between a grunt and a bellow. He stood, his hand going to his Glock. What the hell was that?

And then a cacophony of sound filled the air. Several creatures crying out with the same strange grunting sound. They were distant but coming closer. Loud rustling sounds followed them. And then came a sound that froze his marrow.

"Mack! Pepsy!" he shouted.

"What's going on?" Mack poked her head out of her

tent. Moments later, Pepsy clambered out of his, looking dazed. Both sprang to their feet when they heard the sounds approaching.

"What is that?" Mack asked eyes wide.

Bones grimaced. "Trouble."

14

"**Out of the** tents!" Bones ordered. "We need somewhere to hide." He didn't waste time explaining. The sources of the sounds were rapidly closing in. The explorers were almost out of time.

Bones dashed across the clearing, away from the approaching sounds. His eyes fell on the rotted-out trunk of a mahogany tree. That would have to do.

"All right, elves." He stabbed a finger at the fallen tree. "Everyone inside the hollow tree."

With no hesitation, Mack dove inside. Pepsy wavered, frowned at Bones, and mouthed, "Elves?" Bones rolled his eyes and shoved him roughly inside.

He quickly scooped up two armfuls of fallen leaves and branches, turned, and backed into the hollow tree. Despite its massive girth, it was a tight fit. One inside, he began stuffing the branches and leaves into the narrow crack. It didn't completely fill the open space, but if they were lucky, it would allow them to remain concealed until the danger had passed. Bones prayed that it would mask their scent too.

"What, exactly is coming?" Mack whispered.

As if in answer, a deep bellow rang out and heavy feet thundered forward.

"That sounds like a gorilla," Mack whispered.

More running feet. More thunderous roars.

"They are here!" Pepsy said, his voice trembling with fear.

Despite the perilous situation, Bones couldn't resist taking a peek, Neither could Mack. They peered out from the depths of the rotten tree at the scene unfolding before them.

A troop of gorillas came dashing into the clearing, but these were unlike any gorillas Bones had ever seen.

"My God, they're magnificent," Mack whispered.

It was true. The gorillas were broader of shoulder and at least a head taller than the largest known species of great ape. Their coats were indigo, their silver backs shone in the starlight. But it was not only their size that set them apart. They carried weapons—clubs or cantaloupe-sized rocks. What was more…

"They're communicating," Mack whispered.

The gorillas had come to a halt in the clearing where the trio had camped. One of them, who appeared to be the alpha by the way the others deferred to him, began to vocalize. He grunted at a pair of giant apes, then appeared to point with his lips. The two gorillas grunted back, then headed off in the direction the alpha had indicated. They watched as the gorillas quickly spread out around the clearing.

"What are they doing?" Mack asked.

Bones replied, impressed. "Looks like they're setting a trap."

"A trap? For what?"

From somewhere close by, a high-pitched, ear-splitting cry announced the arrival of something huge as it crashed through the rainforest. Thunderous footsteps shook the ground.

"Mokele-mbembe?" Mack whispered.

Bones shook his head. "I think the legend of the other dinosaur is also true. And I think it's a hunter."

Beyond the tree line, a silhouette appeared, and then a massive foot stamped down on Mack's tent. That was the only glimpse Bones caught of the new dinosaur because the gorillas sprang into action.

Huge stones flew through the air, striking the dinosaur with sick, fleshy splats. Dark shapes flashed back and forth across Bones' field of vision as the gorillas dashed in and out, employing cavalry style hit and run tactics.

They kept the dinosaur at bay at the edge of the clearing. Bones strained to get a glimpse of the creature, but all he could see in the darkness was the occasional flash of reptilian skin. But he could tell the thing was huge. He also caught a glimpse of razor-sharp teeth.

"What do we do?" Mack asked.

"We're doing it. Hopefully, this tree will cover our scent and even hide our heat signature from the dinosaur."

The gorillas had run out of stones and now gave way to the dinosaur. It charged into the clearing and made a beeline for the hollow tree.

"Son of a…"

Bones didn't get the last word out. The dinosaur was on them in a matter of seconds. A trio of giant gorillas charged out to meet it. They clubbed its legs, then leaped beyond the reach of the snapping jaws. The dinosaur whipped its tail around. The gorillas dodged out of the way and its tail struck the hollow tree, chopping it off inches above Bones' head.

"Great hiding place," Mack hissed.

The dinosaur cocked its head, birdlike, and spread its arms, which were surprisingly long. Then it lowered its head and scurried toward the log.

"Holy crap," Bones said. "Looks like it's time for Plan B."

"Plan B?" Mack asked.

"I fight. You two run."

With that, Bones sprang out of the remains of the hollow tree. He clutched his machete in his left hand, and with his right, he aimed his Glock at the dinosaur.

The thing moved on two squat legs. Its crocodilian head was low and narrow, its tail long and lined with sharp spines. Along its back, tall spikes were joined by a membrane, giving it the look of a sail.

Before Bones could fire, its tail whipped around incredibly fast. It caught Bones by the ankle and flipped him into the air. Bones grunted as his hip joint threatened to dislocate, protesting the sudden and violent motion. Flat on his back Bones tensed for it to strike.

But it didn't.

The gorillas, however, did.

Focused on Bones, the dinosaur didn't notice the great apes charge in, striking at its legs. Every strike elicited a shrill cry of pain from it, as well as an angry, grating hiss. The apes paid Bones no attention if they saw him at all.

The dinosaur began to retreat as the full gorilla troop charged in. Suddenly the massive reptile was on the defensive, but it was still in the fight.

"Maybe I can tip the scales." Bones clambered to his feet, took careful aim, and fired off a single shot. It struck the dinosaur right in the snout. Blood flew and it let out a shrill cry. He fired again. This time the bullet glanced off its bony skull. But the dinosaur felt it. It let out a hiss and Bones sent the next slug right into the giant creature's mouth. None of them were killing blows, but they had to hurt.

Bones was prepared to fire again when something rushed past him. Two somethings, in fact.

Mack and Pepsy had joined the fight. They charged in with their machetes, screaming at the top of their lungs. The dinosaur spun around, and the pair hacked at the tip of its tail.

The creature had enough. It let out one last ear-splitting roar, then whipped its tail around to clear away the onlookers. With one last baleful glare that Bones swore was directed at him, it stomped away into the jungle.

Everything went silent. Mack and Pepsy gaped as they realized they stood in the center of a circle of giant, club-wielding gorillas. Pepsy's eyes were like saucers. Mack was white as a sheet.

"What do we do?" Mack whispered.

Bones seldom found himself at a loss for words but right now, he had no idea what to do.

15

The trio stood like statues, frozen in place by the gorillas who seemed to have no more idea what to make of the humans than they had with respect to their hominid cousins. In the distance, Bones could still hear the dinosaur stomping away from them. His heart pounded like a bass drum. He could hear Mack and Pepsy breathing hard.

"Drop your weapons," Bones said, carefully laying his pistol and machete on the ground. Mack and Pepsy let their own machetes fall. He racked his brain for what he knew about gorilla encounters—specifically how to survive them. "Slowly get down on the ground. Make yourselves appear small. And don't look directly at them."

They all sank to the ground, Bones included, and sat hunched over. The gorillas didn't move.

"Any other ideas," Mack said.

"It wouldn't hurt for you to groom each other."

"Groom?"

"Is right," Pepsy said. "I will do it." He reached over and began plucking bits of debris from Mack's hair.

It felt like the longest, most anxious moment of Bones' life. They sat there waiting for the other shoe to fall.

At long last, the alpha let out a grunt and the gorillas turned and headed in the direction opposite the dinosaur. As they melted into the jungle, the alpha turned and looked at Bones. It was only a split second, but as they made eye contact, Bones felt a connection between them. Maybe it was the fact that they were, by the standards of the animal kingdom, closely related. Or, it might have been the simple fact that they had briefly been allies in a battle against a common enemy. The moment was fleeting, but in the end, the apes left them alive, and that was what mattered the most.

When the sounds of the gorilla troop died away, Mack let out a tiny sob and buried her face in her hands. Pepsy raised his hands to the sky, said something in his native tongue, then collapsed in a heap.

Bones couldn't move. He sat there, trying to calm his racing heart, and contemplating their next move. Turning around and going home was probably the wisest move, but it wasn't that simple.

When they had all regained their composure, they huddled in the middle of a dense patch of low growing trees to discuss their situation.

"Do you think those are the gorillas Igor has been studying?" Mack asked.

"Could be," Bones replied. "They really are something else, aren't they?"

"I can't believe they let us go," she said.

"They are wise," Pepsy said. "Not like other apes."

"You knew about them?" Mack demanded.

"Stories," Pepsy simply answered. "Igor once spoke of the Noble Apes."

Bones nodded. The name fit.

"And that dinosaur. What the hell was that thing?" Mack asked.

"It looked like a smaller version of a Spinosaurus," Bones said. Spinosaurus was one of the largest of all carnivorous dinosaurs, even bigger than the T-Rex. The one they had encountered was much smaller than its ancestors. This one stood about five meters tall and maybe ten meters long—just a bit taller than Mokele-mbembe.

"Spin-o-saur-us?" Pepsy asked, slowly sounding it out.

"Spinosaurus was an apex predator living in what is now Northern Africa. She was semi-aquatic, lived, and hunted both in and out of water."

Mack held up a hand. "If we're going to refer to Mokele-mbembe as 'she' can we at least call that asshole 'him?'" She pointed in the direction Spinosaurus had gone.

"Fair enough," Bones said. They lapsed into a brief silence.

"Where do we go now?" Mack asked. "I won't lie. Part of me wants to go home. I've got photos, we've got the scale." Her eyes went wide. "I've got Spinosaurus blood on my machete!" She hastily rummaged into her pack, took out some cotton swabs and glass vials, and began blotting her and Pepsy's machetes. As she worked, she continued to talk. "But another part of me says we're almost there. Less than a day away from Mbanza Mpimpá, tops. We've made it this far, why not go all the way?"

Pepsy let out a low groan.

"I don't think we have a choice," Bones said. He put down the map he'd been studying and spread it out for the others to see. "This is the way back." He traced a line to the west. "But that's the way Spinosaurus went. It also takes us through Mokele-mbembe's territory, and we don't know how far she ranges."

"Which leads us to a second problem," Mack said.

"Exactly. When we parted ways with her, she was headed this way." His finger traced a circle to the south.

"You want to head north and try and circle around Spinosaurus."

Pepsy grunted and shook his head vigorously. "Rebel territory." He tapped a spot to the north. "Very dangerous."

"So, that leaves the lost city," Mack said.

Bones nodded. "Going by Igor's journal, Mbanza Mpimpá is located near the headwaters of a river which eventually feeds back into the branch of the Congo River that we originally came up. We head there, check out the city, then build a raft, and float away."

"Will it keep us clear of angry dinosaurs?" Mack asked.

"I hope so. No promises on hippos, though. They're everywhere."

Mack sighed. "I suppose we'll have to take our chances."

They headed off into the jungle, following the landmarks described in Igor's journal which Bones had plotted onto his own topographical map. Here and there, they came across signs that the gorillas had passed this way.

They were down near the river now, and the way became boggy. Their feet sloshed through the semi-flooded land as they marched onward at a brisk pace. Mosquitoes buzzed around their faces, whining in their ears as they swooped down from above. Soon, the threat of prehistoric creatures was forgotten as they did battle with the mundane annoyances of jungle exploration—mud, heat, humidity, and things that sting and bite.

Bones kept moving full speed. Mack, while tired, was keeping up nicely. Then, there was Pepsy, who seemed to be drained psychologically as well as physically. He was falling behind more and more as the minutes passed.

Silently, he held up a closed fist, signaling for Mack and Pepsy to stop. He pointed over to the cluster of tree trunks and shrubs.

"The river is just over there. I can hear it."

Pepsy nodded, looking awful. "Close to city now I believe."

"Any idea what we can expect to find there?" Bones asked.

"Not sure," Pepsy replied, blinking hard. "Only elders know the place, stories mostly. Last to search for it die many years ago. People go but not return. Except Igor." He rubbed his face hard then fell silent.

"What do you think is there?" Mack asked. "More dinosaurs? Gorillas? Something else?"

Pepsy thought for a moment and then nodded. "Gold."

"How is that dangerous?" Mack asked.

"Gold fever?" Bones asked. "People do crazy things for gold." He doubted it, though. Based on what they had seen and experienced so far, even traveling to the city meant taking your life in your hands.

"Where did the gold come from? Is it mined there?" Mack asked.

"I do not know," Pepsy replied. "Place not talked about. Death and despair."

Bones grimaced. "Sounds like a charming joint." He glanced up at the sky. It was midday. Perhaps they could find a safe place to camp once they had found the city. He consulted his map. Another of Igor's landmarks lay ahead near the river.

He led the way as they slogged through thick vegetation. Several times they disturbed large snakes, but none of them wanted anything to do with the humans who intruded into their domain.

Finally, they reached the river. They saw no sign of hippos, crocodiles, or dinosaurs, so they stripped down to their skivvies and waded in.

The cool water dulled the aches in Bones' joints and dampened his throbbing cuts and bruises. As he scrubbed away the sweat and mud, he felt invigorated. He was ready to find the lost city!

"Hey, Bonebrake," Mack said tentatively. "What is that thing?"

She pointed upriver to something on the near bank.

Bones squinted for a better look and what he saw made his jaw drop.

"What the hell?"

16

Bones' jaw dropped. Sitting on a platform of logs at the river's edge in the shade of the jungle was an old steamboat. It was made of riveted steel, the hull painted red and white. A canopy covered the stern section and an old boiler peeked up from the center.

"It looks like *The African Queen*," Mack said.

"It's pretty old," Bones agreed. "I wonder how long it's been here."

"I hear of this boat," Pepsy said. "Stories say it covered by jungle."

They moved in for a closer look. Bones was surprised to see that it was in excellent condition. The paint was old and faded, but someone had sanded away the rust and had even patched a spot in the hull.

"The canopy is in good shape," Mack observed. "It looks like somebody made it out of an old canvas tent."

Bones reached the bow, where the name *ANASTASIA* had been painted in block letters. Smiling, he vaulted the rail and landed on the deck. It supported his weight easily. He moved to inspect the boiler. It was clean and mostly free of rust. The inside showed signs of a recent fire.

He checked the cargo hold and engine compartment and saw that someone had been maintaining the old steam engine. A small, battered toolbox stood in the corner, and the compartment smelled of oil. He also found a supply of coal set aside for fuel.

"Somebody has been getting this thing ready to run," Bones said.

"I think it was Igor," Mack said. She picked up an engine manual printed in Russian.

"That would explain why the boat is named for a Russian Grand Duchess." Bones paused, thinking of a mission long ago, during his service in the SEALs. He shook his head, refocused his thoughts. "This boat must be his last landmark!" Bones said. "It's in the right spot." Igor had drawn a triangle at a bend in the river. Bones figured it was simply a way to mark the spot on the riverbank, but it could represent the *Anastasia*. "He obviously rediscovered her in the jungle and probably spend years getting her shipshape."

"It's not a complicated engine, is it?" Mack asked. "He could have traded for the things he needed to work on it and carried them in and out." She tapped her chin thoughtfully. Then she brightened. "If this is the last landmark, that means we've almost reached the city."

Bones nodded. Despite his eagerness, he felt a deep sense of foreboding at the thought of finally reaching Mbanza Mpimpá. Then again, could it be any worse than what they had already faced?

They came to a deep, steep-sided depression. The jungle grew right to the edge all around. Bones could see that it was almost perfectly round. A layer of mist hung above the rainforest that covered the floor.

"It looks like a meteorite crater," Mack said. She shielded her eyes from the afternoon sun and squinted down at the treetops far below. "How do we get down there?"

"Same way Igor did," Pepsy said.

"And which way is that?" Bones asked.

"Don't know," Pepsy said, grinning.

Bones stared for a full three seconds before breaking out into laughter. He was quickly shushed by Mack who reminded him that they didn't know what waited for them down below, so perhaps they should approach with a bit more caution.

"The guy finally shows signs of a sense of humor and all you can do is tell me to shut it?" Bones asked.

"How about you two comedians find us a way down to the city."

They circled the edge, looking for a way down. Finally, they came to a narrow footpath that ran alongside a small waterfall. The trail was a steep, switchback worn smooth by many years of erosion. Their heavily laden backpacks made the descent all that much more difficult.

They took their time, choosing their steps with care and pausing a few times for Mack to take photos. They felt like they were walking in a steam bath. Their clothing clung to their skin, from the sweat and humidity. When they finally moved below treetop level and into the shade, they were all overtaken by the chills.

"I can't believe how much cooler it is down here," Mack said. "Darker, too." Although it was late afternoon, it was already twilight in Mbanza Mpimpá.

"Maybe that's why they call it the City of Night," Bones said. "Probably doesn't get very bright down here even at high noon."

"Let's hope that's the only reason," she said.

The path ended at the base of the waterfall where it spilled into a narrow river. Flecks of gold danced beneath the surface of the water, forming into shapes, and bursting apart only to reform again.

"Tell me you're seeing this," Mack said.

"What are you talking about?" Bones deadpanned.

"There's gold in the water," she said. "And it's moving."

"Did you sample some jungle herbs on the way down?"

"I see gold," Pepsy said.

Frowning, Mack raised up on her tiptoes and looked into his eyes. "Are you feeling all right?"

A wide grin split Bones' face. "Just messing with you."

"Ass." She punched him in the ribs, turned, and stalked away.

"You sound like my sister," he grumbled, rubbing the spot where she had struck him. "Except she calls me assclown, sometimes asshat."

"Uriah the Assclown. Sounds like the world's worst court jester."

Pepsy barked a laugh, then flashed an apologetic smile at Bones. "Understand more English than I speak."

"Obviously," Bones said.

"Bonebrake! Come and see this!" Mack called.

"So much for being quiet," Bones mumbled. He joined her at the riverbank, and they knelt at the edge of the water. Up close, Bones could finally see the cause of the phenomenon they had just witnessed. The water teemed with schools of tiny fish, inky black, and striped with bands of shining gold.

"Tetra fish!" Mack whispered. "Thousands of them."

"Like the aquarium fish?" Bones asked.

Mack nodded. "Tetras are common to this region, but I've never seen any that look like this. I want to take some photos and capture a bit of video. You can collect some specimens to take back. There are more jars in my pack." She shrugged off the backpack and handed it to Bones.

"Got a net?" Bones asked.

"Surely, your people know how to catch fish with your bare hands."

"Fully grown fish," Bones said. "Also, that's kind of racist."

"How is it racist for me to express confidence in your ability to do something?" Mack said, taking aim with her camera.

"Would you like it if I expressed confidence in your ability to speak to the manager?"

"Touché," she said. "I'm sorry."

"It's cool. I pegged you as a typical Irish bantam rooster

the moment I saw you. I just never said it out loud."

Mack laughed. "In my case, the stereotype holds true."

"White people always ask if I ride elephant or kill lion," Pepsy said. His smile didn't quite reach his eyes.

"Don't get me started on white people," Bones said, winking at Mack. She gave him the finger and told him to get to work.

With some difficulty, Bones and Pepsy captured several of the tetras. Mack insisted that she photograph them in the process, so when Bones ran afoul of a particularly slippery stone, she managed to snap a few photos of him falling on his ass in the middle of the river.

"That won't make it into Nat Geo," she said, grinning, "but maybe they'll post some outtakes on the website."

"I think my fee just went up," Bones said.

They followed the course of the river as it wound through the dense tropical growth. In short order, they found their way barred by a crumbling stone wall that spanned the narrow river and continued in either direction. It was covered in vines, but a section had been cleared away.

"Looks like somebody took a chunk out of it," Bones said, pointing to chisel marks where someone had carved out a section of wall. The edges were worn smooth. It had been done a long time ago.

Mack frowned, then grabbed a handful of vines to the left of the damaged spot, pulling them away to reveal a petroglyph of a hippo. She dug into her backpack and took out a photograph protected by plastic. It was a printout of the fragment of stele from the royal museum—the one that contained a gorilla petroglyph. She held it up to the empty space on the wall. "What do you think?" she asked.

"Looks like a fit to me." Bones' eyes drifted to the corner of the photograph where a triangular shape ran off the edge of the image. "Wonder what this is a part of." He tapped the triangle.

Mack peeled back more vines. What she uncovered

elicited a groan from Pepsy. The triangular shape was the tip of an animal's tail—a Spinosaurus, to be exact. They cleared away more vines. The Spinosaurus was locked in battle with a Mokele-mbembe.

"This is amazing!" Mack took out her camera and snapped a few photos. When she was finished, she looked at Bones. "Now, how do we get in?"

"We could follow the wall until we find an opening, or we could try to swim underneath it." He inclined his head in the direction of the river where it met the wall. "But I vote we just climb over. It's not that much taller than me."

"Why would they build such a short wall?" Mack asked. "What would be the use?"

"In hand to hand combat, even a wall this size would provide a huge advantage to the defenders. As long as they kept the jungle cleared away, this wall would have made a formidable barrier against invaders."

Mack nodded. "I wonder who they were trying to keep out."

"We don't even know who 'they' were," Bones said.

She reached up and gave him a condescending pat on the cheek. "And that is why we are here. Now, give me and hand up."

Bones laced his fingers together and leaned down so that Mack could step into his cupped hand. He boosted her up and she nimbly clambered up onto the wall where she perched and offered a hand to Pepsy as Bones lifted the guide up.

"I'm not sure we can lift your fat ass up here," Mack said.

Bones didn't need the help. He took a few steps back, got a running start, and jumped. He caught the edge of the wall and swung himself up. It wasn't as graceful as he would have liked, but he managed it.

On the other side of the wall, they found more rainforest. Bones stood atop the barrier and peered deeper into the jungle. Despite the swift approach of night, his sharp eyes spotted something in the distance.

"What do you see?" Mack asked.

He smiled. "Gold."

17

In the fading light, Bones could just make out a golden glow in the distance. The trio clambered down off the wall and, using their machetes, hacked their way through the jungle growth. They soon encountered hilly terrain.

"Something about this feels alien," Mack said, slashing a thick vine in two.

It only took Bones a minute to understand. The hills they encountered were too perfectly round, well-aligned, and evenly spaced. Each was surmounted by a single ancient tree, which was encircled by multiple rings of vegetation. He soon realized what he was looking at.

"These aren't hills. They're structures. At least, they were." Most of them were just piles of rubble, caving in on themselves over time, ruined by the natural elements. Whoever used to call this place home no longer did.

Mack paused, squinted, and then gave a nod. "I can see it now. It almost looks like they were terraced with trees and plants growing on top." Natural camouflage. It was an ingenious way to hide what someone, or something, didn't want to be found. "Very resourceful. I'm curious to know how it was done." She motioned to the canopy above them.

Bones nodded. "And whether the complex was always intended to be hidden away from the world, or if it was done after the fact."

"Trees like this," Pepsy added, "take generations to grow. Very old."

Bones stood. "It's getting late. Let's get a move on."

Slowly, the three of them moved forward. There was just enough sunlight coming through to light their way. With the afternoon sun shining in, they easily worked their way between the collapsed buildings. As they drew closer to the golden light, the way grew easier, with only low growing foliage to bar their way.

"Do you think somebody's been maintaining part of the city?" Mack asked.

Bones shrugged. His eyes and thoughts were on the glowing object in front of them. He could see now that it was a golden block of some sort, built upon an earthen mound and sheltered by the tallest mahogany tree Bones had ever seen. He estimated the tree was more than thirty meters tall—well over one hundred feet.

They approached the mound. A set of stairs ran up the circular hill. Bones held out a hand for Mack and Pepsy to stay back. Taking the steps two at a time, Bones reached the top and found himself standing in front of a golden altar.

A sacrificial altar.

It was almost rectangular in shape—slightly wider at the head and narrower at the foot. He had just seen something similar while in Cabras—altars of gold. Unlike its Sardinian counterparts—this altar was carved from a single block of quartz inlaid with thick veins of golden yellow. Bones had seen enough gold in his time to know that this was the real thing and not pyrite, so-called "fool's gold," which tended to be brassy in color. Also, unlike Cabras, this altar wasn't slathered in dried blood.

He slid his hand across the pristine surface, marveling at its perfection. No crack or chip marred its surface. Each side of the altar was carved with the image of a different creature: Spinosaurus on one side, Mokele-mbembe on the side opposite, a gorilla at the foot. But it was the image below the head of the altar that made him suck in a sharp breath.

The thing had the powerful body of a gorilla, but large eyes, flat face, and protruding ears of a chimpanzee. It bared its pointed teeth and seemed to glare at Bones. Pointed teeth? He wondered if it were a matter of artistic license, or if this were an accurate representation of another undiscovered ape. Bones had a bad feeling about everything so far, and this was just adding to his spiking paranoia.

"Bones!" Mack said in a whisper. "What do you see?"

"Come on up and take a look."

Mack and Pepsy joined him and gave the altar a thorough inspection. All agreed that this was unlike anything ever discovered in this region. Perhaps the people that constructed this place were a distinct, isolated culture. They needed to investigate the buildings and see if they could find any artifacts that would help tell the story of this place.

He stood and turned in a slow circle, but there was little to see. The altar was surrounded by collapsed buildings that had succumbed to the jungle's relentless approach.

"We've found Mbanza Mpimpá and I have more questions than answers," Mack said. "Who built this place? Why did they choose this spot? Did the crater have anything to do with it? Who or what were they sacrificing? When did it all stop?"

Bones nodded. "And what was Igor so afraid of?"

With that grim thought in their minds, they decided to bed down for the night. They found a nearby building that was still intact. It was round, three-tiered, and reminded Bones of a wedding cake. Jungle growth covered the roofs of each level and a tree stump protruded from the highest point.

"I guess the tree died before it destroyed the building beneath it," Mack said.

Load-bearing stone walls divided the first floor into seven pie-shaped rooms. All were empty, save for dirt and debris. At the center, a hole in the ceiling led up to the second level. The broken remains of what had once been a ladder lay on the floor.

"I'd really like to check out the higher levels," Bones said.

"I don't think we can boost you up," Mack said. "But you could probably lift me up."

"I don't know," Bones said.

"You don't think I can do it?" she asked.

"It's not that. I just feel like I ought to go first in case there's something dangerous up there."

"Just lift me up high enough that I can see over the ledge. If anything looks out of sorts, you can drop me right back down." When Bones hesitated, she added, "I am your boss. Remember?"

Chuckling, Bones relented. He lifted Mack up until she could reach the second floor. She shone her light around.

"Looks pretty much the same as the first floor, but smaller," she said. "This level isn't as wide, and the ceiling is only about six feet high. Each room has a narrow window, like an arrowslit in a castle. They're mostly covered in vegetation."

"No artifacts?" Bones asked.

"Nothing. But I'll check out the third floor." Before Bones could object, she pushed herself up, stepping on Bones' head as she clambered through.

"Don't you need a ladder?" Bones asked, brushing the dirt out of his hair.

"Nope. There's a step up, and the ceiling is quite low. Just a second."

Bones took a step back. At this angle, he could see her legs. They were blotchy and sunburned, but quite shapely. He saw Pepsy leering at her.

"Come on, dude. She's our boss." The two men stared at each other, then broke out into laughter. The moment of brevity was cut off an instant later by Mack's scream.

18

"Mack!" Bones shouted. He leaped up toward the second floor opening and caught hold of the ledge. Grunting, he began pulling himself up. "Pepsy, give me a lift!"

Pepsy ducked beneath him, positioned Bones' feet on his shoulders, and stood to his full height. He wasn't particularly tall, but it more than did the job. Bones scrambled up and sprang to his feet.

Pain burst in his skull as something struck him on top of the head. He saw stars and he staggered backward.

"Bones!" Mack shouted. He heard footsteps and then her arms were around his waist, pulling him toward her. "You almost fell back through the hole."

He peered at her through watery eyes. "Did you hit me?"

"Of course I didn't. You forgot what I said about the low ceiling up here."

Bones' ears were ringing and his head hurting far too much to be embarrassed at his blunder. He hoped he wasn't concussed, mostly because it was a stupid way to get injured.

"Why did you scream?" he asked, remembering why he had climbed up in the first place.

"Oh, that." Mack glanced away. "Sorry, I saw a skeleton and it scared me."

"A skeleton," Bones repeated.

"It's really messed up. You'll understand when you see it." Her tone held a note of defensiveness.

"Okay, I'll check it out," Bones said, looking up at the hole in the ceiling that led to the third and highest level.

"Watch your head." Mack flashed a wicked smile.

Bones made his best attempt at a roguish grin, but a

burst of pain in his head turned it into a grimace. He mounted the stone step and stuck his head and shoulders through the opening. Even knowing what to expect, he winced when his light fell on the skeleton. It was as messed up as Mack had said.

It was the skeleton of a gorilla. Not that of one of the giants with whom they had crossed paths, but still of respectable size. The skull, however, was clearly not that of a gorilla. Its jaw was slightly smaller, its cranium larger, and it lacked the sagittal crest—the ridge of bone that ran along the middle of the top of the skull. It was a chimpanzee skull.

"Remember that weird ape that was carved below, the head of the altar?" Mack asked. "I think you found it."

Bones climbed up for a closer look, this time being careful not to hit his head on the low ceiling. He gave Mack a hand up, and they moved in for a closer inspection of the skeleton. Bones immediately noticed that, like the carving on the altar, the ape had sharp, pointed teeth.

"It's weird," he said, focusing his light on the lower jaw. "This thing has no incisors, no bicuspids, no molars. Evolutionarily, it doesn't make sense."

"Maybe they were vampires?" Mack said.

Bones chuckled. "Well, at least this guy isn't sparkly."

And then a glint of metal caught his eye. And another. The ape's wrists and ankles were shackled to the wall with heavy iron chains and cuffs. The thing had been a captive!

"This gets weirder and weirder," Mack said. "How do you even capture a thing like that, much less get him up to the third floor. And why?"

"I think he was injured when they caught him." Bones pointed to the right leg, where both the tibia and fibula showed obvious signs of a badly healed break. "If he couldn't move well, they could have caught him in a net, maybe even drugged him. As for getting him up here, maybe some kind of pulley?" He directed his light up to the ceiling, where a rusted iron chain hung.

"Well, aren't we the smart one?" Mack said.

"I've had to incapacitate and imprison some big dudes in my time."

"In the service or in your civilian life?" Mack asked.

Bones waggled his hand. "A bit of this, a bit of that."

Mack returned to the bottom floor for her camera and she began making a thorough record of the room. It wasn't long before the bright flashes brought something to Bones' attention.

"Petroglyphs!" He pointed to a spot on the wall opposite the ape skeleton. The jungle had crept in through the arrowslit window in the wall and obscured carvings in the stone. He and Mack carefully cleared away the vines.

The petroglyphs were carved into the blocks of dark stone from which the building was constructed. The first one he saw showed a group of people kneeling around a large circle.

"The crater," Mack said softly.

"Yep." Bones had thought the exact same thing. "If this really was caused by a meteorite, then the people who built this city might have worshipped it as a gift from the gods."

"Or as a god, even," Mack added.

Bones nodded then returned his attention to the precisely carved images. The next one showed those same people grouped around what looked like a stone. Those closest to it lay dead. Others shielded their eyes.

"Radioactive?" Mack asked.

"Could be," Bones said.

The third pictograph shed further light on the history of the city. Alien looking people, with thick, oddly shaped bodies and what appeared to be beams of light radiating from them, were depicted building some sort of vault around the meteorite. It was then covered in an earthen mound with an altar atop it.

Bones and Mack exchanged looks. "We were literally right on top of the meteorite."

Bones knew what she was thinking. Had they been exposed to deadly levels of radiation? His gut told him no, but they couldn't be certain. Nothing they could do about it except hope the aliens, or whatever they were, knew what they were doing when they enclosed the meteorite. Also, he planned on departing this valley as soon as it was safe. Once it was light, Mack could snap some photos and they'd get the hell out of Dodge.

The next petroglyph was grim. It showed a person lying on the altar, awaiting sacrifice. There was no sign of the strange, glowing people.

"I'm confused," Mack said. "They made sacrifices to the meteorite?"

Bones shrugged. "Does the story continue?"

They looked around but found no more petroglyphs.

"Maybe we'll learn the rest of the story when we explore the city," Mack said.

After one final search, they bedded down for the night. They did so on the second level, reasoning that it would be safer in the event that they weren't alone in the valley.

They ate a cold meal of protein bars and slices of the African mango that grew wild in the Congo basin. While they dined, they read through Igor's journal.

"I don't suppose you can read French," Mack said.

"Screw the French," Bones said.

Mack rolled her eyes, then returned to the journal. With Pepsy's aid, they translated the words drawn from regional languages, and each knew a smattering of French, and through context clues and guesswork, they navigated their way through that language as well. Bones' one contribution was "zoloto," the Russian word for gold.

Finally, Mack went pale. "I think I figured out what Igor was so afraid of."

"The meteorite?" Bones asked. "Spinosaurus? Being forced to use leaves for toilet paper?"

She managed a wan smile. "I think it has to do with our

friend on the third floor."

Bones stiffened. He had hoped the skeleton represented an extinct species.

Mack raised the journal and began to read aloud.

"*Remarkably, the entrance to the temple is not hidden in any way, save for the intrusion of the rainforest that shields it from sight. This suggests that the people of Mbanza Mpimpá made regular use of it in some way. Was it a place of public worship? Perhaps it was the domain of the priestly class. I shall learn more in the morning.*"

She looked up at Bones.

"Don't keep me in suspense. Where's the temple? What did he find?"

"He doesn't say. In fact, the next dated entry is weeks later, and he never mentions the lost city again."

"Does he say anything at all?"

"Only this." Mack flipped the journal around so that Bones could see the entry. Three words were scrawled across the page.

"*Singe de sang,*" he read aloud. "What does that mean?"

"It's French," she said. "Loosely translated, it means Blood Ape."

19

They rose early, as soon as the first rays of light touched the forest canopy. They were eager to explore. And, although no one said it, they were all tense. The fact that the fastidious Igor hadn't recorded anything about his exploration of the temple was unsettling. And what about these so-called "Blood Apes" had frightened him so much that he preferred an encounter with Mokele-mbembe to a return to the crater.

They made a quick inspection of the ruined buildings. Virtually all had been reduced to rubble. The few that still stood, even partially, were empty. No artifacts and certainly no gold lying everywhere.

"This is weird," Mack said. "Do you think whoever it was just packed up and left?"

"It's possible," Bones said. "But in a scenario like that, things get left behind. We haven't found a single artifact."

"Any other ideas, then?" Mack asked.

"Maybe it wasn't a place where people lived year-round. They might have made pilgrimages here. You're less likely to leave your garbage behind in a sacred place." He paused. "Well, people back then respected sacred spaces."

Mack nodded. "I think we've seen everything except this mysterious temple. I say we check it out."

Bones brushed the sweat from his forehead and looked up at the sky. Though it was late morning, the sky was turning gray.

"Looks like a storm is rolling in," he said. A distant peal of thunder underscored his words.

Mack looked up at the sky and nodded. "In that case, I don't think we should try climbing out of the crater until it passes over. That trail is precarious enough as it is."

Bones couldn't disagree. What was more, he didn't want to leave without exploring the temple. To come all this way, risk death time and again, and leave a major portion of the city unexplored? He couldn't do it.

"There has been no sign of the Blood Apes," Mack offered, misinterpreting his silence.

"All right, Red. We'll check it out. But if at any point I say we have to turn back, you do it with no argument."

For a moment, he thought she would argue, but finally, she nodded. "I don't want to meet the thing that frightens you enough to make you want to turn back."

"Just hope Angelina Jolie isn't waiting down there. You'd probably get away, but she would definitely try and adopt me and Pepsy."

"I thought you speak no French, Mister Bone," Pepsy said. "Who is the pretty angel?"

"No, that's a person's name," Bones said. "Never mind. We've got a temple to find."

Igor was correct. It was easy to find the entrance to the temple now that they knew there was one to look for. They found it on the back side of the earthen mound, hidden beneath a curtain of vines and long grasses. It was a stone door without lock or key.

"Here goes nothing," Bones said. He threw his shoulder against the door. It gave way slowly, with a dull scraping sound, to reveal stone steps that spiraled down into the darkness. Another thunderclap, this one much closer, boomed out.

The air inside was cool and musty. A whiff of a foul odor made him crinkle his nose. They confirmed that the door had no latch, then let it close behind them. They stood there in silence for a moment, listening, but the only thing Bones heard was his companions' rapid breathing. They were more frightened than they let on.

Finally, Bones took out his flashlight and flicked it on.

He longed for his Mini-Maglite, but Igor's old-school model did in a pinch. Mack and Pepsy produced their own lights, and the stairwell was bathed in light.

The staircase was constructed of black stone, all of which sparkled with glittering gold. The walls and ceilings were lined with polished quartz. The reflected light made it seem bright as day.

The height of the ceiling and the breadth of the steps caught Bones' attention. Judging by what they had seen already, the dimensions were much larger than what would be needed for the people who built this city. Perhaps the builders were larger than the natives?

"How long did it take them to build this place?" Mack asked quietly as they descended the stairs. They instinctively spoke in hushed tones, although they had no reason to believe they were not alone.

"No idea. Hundreds of years?" Bones replied.

She paused to take a photograph. "Why a temple, though? They buried the meteorite safely. They added the altar on top for religious purposes. So, why this underground temple?

That was a good question. Bones knew how the minds of men worked. When it came to places of worship, some built them out of devotion to, or fear of their deity. But places of worship like this could have more sinister uses. Conditioning a populace to participate in unified rituals and hold to a single religion was a useful way of controlling their thoughts and actions. And in some cases, a place like this reflected an individual or society's desire to leave its mark.

"Could be superstition," he began, "or politics, or ego."

"Ego?" Mack replied.

"Okay, maybe that's the wrong word. They wanted to leave their mark on the world, and maybe this temple is it?"

"Why bury it, then?"

Bones shrugged. "Not sure. Maybe the aliens told them

to do it."

The stairs ended at what Bones figured was five stories or around fifty feet. Whatever created the impact crater, it was now buried deep. Before them lay a long corridor. In the distance, their lights glinted off the surface of something gold.

"What could that be?" Mack whispered.

"Only one way to find out."

The golden glow proved to be four of the oddest suits Bones had ever seen. The suits consisted of a gourd-shaped, gold-plated helmet with a single, narrow eye-slit, a leather vest covered with thin gold foil, and what looked like leather chaps covered with the same fine sheets of gold. Each hung from a faceless stone statue.

"They don't look alien," Mack said.

Bones laughed and clapped himself on the forehead. It was so obvious now. "That's because they weren't aliens. Gold blocks most radiation, and this crater supposedly had plenty of it."

"They made their own anti-radiation suits so they could safely deal with the meteorite!" Mack said. She snapped a few photos and they moved on.

They turned a corner and found themselves face to face with a Spinosaurus. Mack gasped and sprang back, her hand going to her machete.

"Just a statue," Bones said. Damn, the thing was lifelike. "Let's see what's on the other side." Heart in his throat, he rounded the statue and froze. "Holy freaking crap."

20

Before them lay a heaping pile of gold. It was mounded up around the base of a cube-shaped, gold-plated vault about five meters square. This was where the meteorite had been sealed away. The floor, walls, and ceiling were made from polished black stone.

They moved into the chamber and circled the mound of gold. Some of the nuggets were the size of his fist.

"Why did they bring all their gold down here?" Mack said.

"Isolated tribe, maybe they didn't engage in commerce."

"In which case the gold would be more valuable as an insulator than anything else," Mack said. It was an incredible revelation.

They moved closer and Bones scooped up and handful popcorn-sized nuggets. It was some of the purest gold he had ever seen.

Mack let out a gasp. She pointed at something a few meters away. A human skull peeked up from the mound of gold. And then he realized that there was much more than gold piled around the sides of the vault. Mixed within the booty were many bones. From the shape and length of the corpses, Bones knew he was looking at human remains.

"What the hell?" she asked.

Nearby lay a rib cage. Bones pocketed his handful of gold, then worked the rib cage free so he could examine it. He could immediately tell that the heart had been cut out. "Sacrifice," he said, showing her the long grooves in the bone. "But it's weird. The cuts are rough, like the job was done hastily."

"I would guess these are the bodies that were sacrificed

on the altar upstairs," she said, "but it's hard to believe that the people who built the golden altar with such care and precision would take such a hack and slash approach to sacrifice."

Bones agreed. It was puzzling. He picked up a femur and let out a surprised grunt. The bone was covered in teeth marks.

"Somebody ate this dude," he said. "Straight off the bone, too."

"Cannibalism?" she asked.

Bones shook his head. The cannibals of which he was aware tended to treat a human corpse the same as the remains of any other game animal. They would dress the body and prepare the meat. He would expect to see cut marks on the victim's bones, but no bite marks.

They continued to examine the pile of gold. The nuggets comprised only the top layer of what was piled around the vault. Much of what lay below was quartz with only specks of gold inside, and there was a generous amount of the black sand found at the bottom of the river outside the city walls.

"That's a long way to carry heavy sand," Mack said.

"That doesn't seem to have been a consideration to the ancients," Bones said. "Look at Stonehenge, the pyramids."

Mack nodded. "Never underestimate the power of devotion," she said. "Or a ruler's willingness to work slaves and subjects to death," she added.

Bones didn't reply. He had just made a new discovery.

There were more skeletal remains buried beneath the black sand, but these were not human. They were Blood Apes. He recognized the chimpanzee-like skulls with their sharp fangs. As he dug deeper, he found more Blood Ape bones, but the ape buried the deepest did not have a mouthful of pointed teeth, but instead had a relatively normal array, though the molars were few and the incisors were sharp and came to a point like a shovel. A theory forming in his mind, he moved to the far end of the vault and began to dig. Sure enough, the skeletal remains he found on top were human. One leg bone still had bits of flesh attached to it. It couldn't be more than a few months old. He crinkled his nose and kept digging.

As he had expected, as he went deeper, he found only Blood Ape skeletons. He was about to inform Mack of his discovery when she let out a yelp. He hurried over to the far side of the vault. She pointed a trembling finger at the gold pile. Partially buried lay the fresh corpse of one of Igor's Noble Apes. Its heart had been cut out.

A cold certainty rose inside of him. Bones thought he knew what was going on. He explained what he had found.

"You think the people who lived here started out sacrificing Blood Apes and only turned to human sacrifice after they eradicated that population? And now they're sacrificing the Noble Apes?"

That was not exactly what he was thinking, but she was on the right track. But before he could explain, a foul wind blew over him. He and Mack covered their noses and turned to see where the breeze had come from. Between the darkness and their interest in the gold, they had failed to notice a door set in the stone.

While Mack took photographs of the temple area, Bones moved in for a closer look. He eased the door open and shone his light inside. A passageway led back into the darkness, and from it, a musky, pungent scent emanated. It smelled like an animal's den. That couldn't be good.

Wondering what else they had missed, he took a few steps back and gave the temple a second look. He panned his light around, searching higher on the walls until something caught his eye. Up above the passageway through which they had entered, there was a gaping hole in the wall where some of the stones had been removed. He thought he could see a passageway on the other side. In the corner, he spotted another opening with a corridor behind it. And then another.

"Holy freaking crap." Bones couldn't believe his own stupidity. He should have given the temple a thorough inspection before poking around in the gold heap. And then his sharp ears heard something coming from the tunnel directly above the entrance. It was a deep grunt.

Pepsy heard it, too. "Mister Bone, something is coming."

"Red, I think we should go."

21

Mack sprang to her feet. Her heart was racing and her senses were all on high alert. "What's going on?"

"Something is coming," Bones said.

They hadn't taken three steps toward the exit when a cacophony of sound burst from the corridor through which they had entered. Many somethings were coming! Bones didn't speak. He grabbed the other two by the wrist and hauled them back to the door he'd discovered moments before.

They slipped inside, pulled the door almost shut, and turned out their flashlights. As Bones peered through the crack, he saw something he hadn't noticed before. Four thin beams of light shone down from the ceiling, one from each point of the compass. The four beams met atop the golden vault. The light was so wan that their flashlights had completely overpowered it. Now, with no other light source, they seemed like laser beams. A circle of golden light provided enough illumination for Bones to watch as the scene played out.

Apes began to peer out from the holes up above. Finally, they got their first good look at a Blood Ape. They were a twisted blend of gorilla and chimp. They stood half a head shorter than the Noble Apes. Their builds were less muscular, their arms longer. And, as the skeleton had indicated, they had chimpanzee-like heads and pointed teeth.

They bared sharp teeth and let out angry grunts. From the entrance came another group of the same, horrific creatures. Some were armed with clubs or carried sharp stones. Others dashed back and forth, pounding their chests, slapping the walls.

"What are they doing?" Mack said.

"It looks like they're preparing for a sacrifice," Bones said. "In any case, it doesn't look like we can go back the way we came."

"Looks like there's only one other choice," Mack said, glancing over her shoulder. "But that might just take us deeper into danger."

"If there's no way out, maybe we can at least find somewhere to hide. We're exposed right here."

Mack nodded. "I really want to take a photograph of this."

Bones raised a finger in warning. "Don't you freaking dare." When she gave a reluctant nod, he smiled. "Well, then," he said, starting off, "into the darkness we go."

"Again..."

Bones smiled. Mack was growing on him. They felt their way around a bend in the passageway and then Mack flicked on her red-tinted beam. It provided sufficient light for them to see that this passageway was not made by human hands, although it had been improved. It was a naturally formed passage that angled almost imperceptibly upward. The way had been cleared of debris, and in some places, stones had been chipped away to form a smooth path.

The image of Blood Apes moving up and down the passageway flashed across his mind. The beasts used this path regularly, he was sure of it. If they weren't careful, he and Mack could literally walk into the "belly of the beast."

As they moved along, the odor grew stronger. Bones thought he knew why. "I think their den is this way," he said.

"Gorillas don't live in dens, do they?" Mack asked.

"They also don't perform ritual sacrifices in temples full of gold, but here we are."

Up ahead, the way grew brighter. Bones sensed a large,

open space ahead. The corridor ended moments later, revealing an opening ahead that was lit from within. The light rolled like a reflection off roiling water.

"It looks like natural sunlight," Mack announced, stunned.

With practiced caution, Bones crept forward, laying himself flat against the inside of the doorway. Mack did the same on the right-hand side.

It was a large chamber. Faint light filtered down from somewhere high above, and water dripped from the ceiling and gathered in a pool at the center. On the opposite side, the pathway continued. All around were what could only be called dungeon cells—large alcoves hewn from the rock and enclosed by thick iron bars.

"Who were they keeping here?" Mack asked.

Bones stepped out into the cavern and looked around. Why would the people who built Mbanza Mpimpá have put cells down here? And then he remembered the skeletons piled around the base of the vault. They had all been Blood Apes.

"I think I understand," he said. "The people here started out sacrificing Blood Apes. Those were the only skeletons I found on the bottom layer. I think this is where they were held."

Mack took out her camera and snapped a photograph. At the first flash, something close by bellowed so loudly that Bones jumped a foot off the floor. Mack let out a shriek and drew her machete. Bones trained his Glock in the direction of the sound. The sound came again, lower this time, but it came no closer.

"Shine your light over there," he told Mack. She did as he said. Trapped inside a cell was one of the Noble Apes. Bones recognized him immediately by the beardlike streak of silver that lined his jaws and chin. "It's the alpha."

"Oh my God. Do you think the Blood Apes are planning on sacrificing him?"

Before Bones could reply, an easily identifiable grunting sound reverberated around them, causing Bones to grit his teeth. It was the low grunts of great apes, and they sounded agitated.

Mack went pale. "The Blood Apes are coming."

22

The Blood Apes were coming for their sacrifice! The grunts and slapping sounds grew louder. They would be here soon, and Bones had nowhere near enough bullets to take them all down. They had to get out of here.

The Noble Ape began to vocalize, but it was not the angry bellow of before. It carried a pleading tone. The ape beckoned him forward.

"We can't leave him here," Bones said.

Pepsy let out a low moan. "It will kill us, Mister Bone."

"He let us go once before. I don't think he means to hurt us." Bones locked eyes with the gorilla. A bad idea in most cases, but he could see the intelligence in the giant ape's eyes. Before he could change his mind, he headed for the cell.

"Are you sure about this?" Mack asked, falling in beside him.

"No, but if I were a betting man, and I am, this is the play I would make."

"Me too," she said. "I figure we're probably going to die anyway, so a little added karma won't go amiss."

Pepsy began to whimper.

"If you don't like it, the way out is that way." Bones pointed to the corridor on the other side of the cavern. "At least I hope it's the way out, or else we're all really screwed."

"I will stay," Pepsy said. He held his machete out in front of him like a rapier and turned to face the passageway that led back to the temple.

They hurried over to the cell. The ape, seeming to sense their hesitation, backed away from the bars and let out a low grunt.

"Here goes nothing," Bones said.

"I get the feeling you say that a lot," Mack replied.

A thick beam of mahogany barred the cell door. At one end, beyond the reach of any prisoner, an iron pin fastened the beam to the stone wall. Bones removed the pin and he and Mack tried to work it free. It barely moved. The gorilla bellowed.

"We're working on it!" Bones snapped. "We aren't as strong as you guys."

As if understanding, the ape came to the front of the cell. The entire scene was so surreal that neither Bones nor Mack flinched. The ape seized hold of the bar and pushed. Because of the narrow bars, he could only budge it an inch, but it made all the difference. Once the wooden beam, worn smooth with age, began sliding, Bones and Mack were able to remove it. Bones took a deep breath and opened the door.

The Noble Ape scrambled out of the cell on all fours and shot across the cavern. He stopped at the corridor that led out, turned, and bellowed.

"Was that a thank you?" Mack asked.

The gorilla bellowed again and pointed with his lips toward the exit.

"I think it's an invitation. Let's go."

The trio took off, following the Noble Ape up the passageway. Behind them, the noise of the approaching Blood Apes grew louder. It wouldn't be long before they discovered their sacrifice was missing. And there was only one direction they could run.

The tunnel twisted and turned, slowing their progress. The gorilla could move much faster than the humans, but the narrow corridor slowed him down enough for Bones to keep him in sight.

"It can't be much farther, can it?" Mack said.

"I think we're well beyond the walls of the crater, and we've been climbing for a while."

More shrieks and howls rang out, seemingly right behind them. The Blood Apes were closing in. Pepsy yelped but kept running.

"Tell me we're going to make it," Mack said.

"Don't worry. I've got your back," Bones said. He was wondering how long it would be before he was forced to make a last stand.

Finally, he saw a glimmer of light up ahead, caught a whiff of fresh air. They were almost back to the surface!

They sprinted up a narrowing corridor and broke out into a steep-sided box canyon. The walls sloped in on all sides, and the jungle hung over the edges, leaving only a small circle of angry gray sky visible. Lightning flashed and thunder rolled.

"What are those?" Mack panted.

In alcoves high on the canyon walls were what looked like giant bird's nests. Chimpanzees and other great apes built their dens, called "nests," in the boughs of trees. There was only low growth in this canyon, so the Blood Apes had utilized rock overhangs.

"I think we're trespassing in their neighborhood," he said.

"Why are you smiling?" she asked, eyes wide with terror.

"I was just thinking how much this reminds me of the Mesa Verde cliff dwellings."

"Why is that funny?"

"It's a new species so it needs a new name. Like the Ape-nasazi."

"I'm going to pretend I didn't hear that."

They reached the opposite wall of the canyon. The Noble Ape stopped and pointed to handholds carved in the rock. Pepsy didn't have to be told twice. He immediately began climbing.

Behind them, the high-pitched cries of the Blood Apes rang out. Bones whirled around. A half dozen emerged into the canyon. They paused for a moment, then the leader spotted Bones and the others. The creature let out a howl and pounded his chest. It grunted something to its companions. One of them plunged back into the tunnel while the rest took off in pursuit of the fleeing intruders.

"Well, damn," Bones said, watching as they barreled toward him. He drew his Glock then patted his pocket to find the spare magazine. He glanced over his shoulder and saw that Mack had begun to climb. But the apes were closing in fast. Too fast.

"Bonebrake! What are you doing?" Mack shouted.

"Remember Plan B?" he asked, his voice dull.

"You fight; we run? Dammit, Bonebrake. Don't be a hero."

"Don't worry about me," Bones said. "I'll catch up."

23

The Noble Ape let out a grunt and prodded him with a massive finger. Even he seemed to sense the urgency of the situation.

"I'm coming," Bones said. "Just give me a second to see if I can slow them down. Cover your ears."

He didn't know if the Noble Ape understood him, or simply remembered how loud the pistol had been, but he covered his ears with his giant hands.

Five apes. Bones knew he couldn't take many of them out, but if he could disable a couple of the leaders, that might buy him some time. They charged in running on all fours. The low profile gave little in the way of a vulnerable target—mostly thick skull and powerful shoulders and chest. He'd have to get it just right to do any real damage. He dropped to one knee, took careful aim, and squeezed off a pair of shots in quick succession.

The lead ape let out a banshee shriek and fell face-first to the ground. It tumbled head over heels and landed in a heap, clutching its groin.

"No freaking way," Bones said. He'd been aiming for the gut but must have caught the ape in mid-leap.

The ape just behind the leader was taken by surprise and stumbled across his fallen companion. He only stayed down for a few seconds before scrambling back to his feet and rejoining the attack.

Bones fired two shots at each ape, then quickly changed magazines. No time to assess the damage. The apes were almost on top of them.

And then something yanked him up by the belt and he was slowly rising through the air. It took him a second to realize what was happening. The Noble Ape was carrying him up the cliff. Facing backward and staring down at the canyon floor, he felt like a baby in a carrier.

"Dude, you are strong. Do you work out?" Bones said. The ape grunted. "Man, I wish I spoke your language."

The Blood Apes were huddled at the bottom of the wall. Every one of them appeared to be nursing an injury of some sort and were reluctant to continue the pursuit.

"I think they're giving up," Bones said.

But then more howls echoed through the canyon. An entire troop of Blood Apes burst into the clearing, shrieking with rage. They saw Bones and the others, and their shrieks grew more strident. The largest of them, a graying ape, held up a sharpened stick and let out a series of whoops. The others echoed him. And then they charged.

"Will I ever catch a break?" Bones muttered. "I'll keep them off our backs," he said loudly. The ape grunted again. *Either he got the gist, or he wants me to shut up.*

One of the Blood Apes flung his sharpened stick at Bones. Bones would have thought they were out of range, but the ape was so powerful that the primitive spear flew true. Bones gritted his teeth as he watched it fly toward him. At the last second, he swatted at it with the Glock and manage to bat it aside.

The near-miss inspired the other Blood Apes. Moments later, a hail of sticks and rocks flew through the air. Bones made himself as small a target as possible, covered his head, and hoped for the best. The first several projectiles fell short of their mark. Bones could hear them clattering off the face of the canyon below him.

But they didn't all miss their target. They rained down all around. A rock bounced off his shoulder, and then pain like a hot poker burned in his thigh. He opened his eyes to see one of the sharpened sticks jutting from his leg.

"Son of a…" He gritted his teeth, grabbed hold of it, and gave it a yank. With no spearhead or barbed tip, the primitive weapon came free easily. "Missing something?" He reversed the spear and hurled it down into the midst of the Blood Apes.

Bones and his rescuer were now out of missile range. The apes scrambled to the cliff wall and several began to climb. One of them took the lead, howling and shrieking. Its eyes burned and spittle ran from the corners of its mouth. It quickly closed the gap between them. Bones had no choice.

"It's about to get loud!" he shouted. Even as he took aim, he felt a wave of guilt at even attempting to take this rare creature's life. But right now, it was kill or be killed, and there were a lot of things and people Bones had not yet done. He took aim, not an easy task, being carried like he was. The ape closed in. Bones squeezed the trigger.

The shot took the ape in the eye. Its cries were abruptly cut off. It froze in place for a second. Then, its body went limp. Like a tree being chopped down, it slowly tipped backward and fell. Which was unfortunate for two more Blood Apes who failed to get out of the way. The corpse struck them on the way down and sent them plummeting to the ground.

That caused the others to hesitate. The few extra seconds was enough. Bones felt himself hauled up over the edge of the cliff. He stood and immediately stumbled as pain shot down his leg.

"You're hurt," Mack said.

"It'll be fine," he said. He turned back toward the cliff face, intending to continue the fight. The Noble Ape, however, turned him around and gave him a shove along a faint path that sloped down into the jungle. Bones hesitated.

"Come on," Mack said, taking him by the arm. "I think he's got this."

The huge gorilla had uprooted a small tree. He raised it high above his head, let out a roar, and hurled it downward. They heard the fading shriek of a falling Blood Ape.

"You're right. He's got this." They headed off down the path. Pepsy took the lead. The man's wide eyes, rapid breathing, and trembling hand said he was reaching his limit and couldn't wait to be free of this place. He dashed forward, hacking wildly with his machete.

Lightning flashed so close by that the hair on Bones' arms stood up. The shock of white light was followed by a boom of thunder like cannon fire. Bones felt the vibrations from his fillings to his feet. Rain began to fall. The storm was upon them.

"Where do you think the trail leads?" Mack panted as they stumbled along.

"Down to the river," Bone said. He could hear the rush of the water somewhere down below. They were getting close. To his right, he heard something crashing through the jungle, headed their way. He immediately thought of several possibilities, none of them good.

"What is that?" Mack asked.

"Almost certainly bad news."

Then a graying Blood Ape broke into the clear right in front of them. It was the one Bones had identified as the alpha—older, larger, and just a bit more insane than the rest. It stood on its hind legs, roared, and beat its chest. Bones didn't hear any other apes chasing them. This one must have climbed up a different way and flanked them. Now it barred their way.

"Any bright ideas?" Mack said.

Bones shook his head. "Only reckless ones."

24

The enraged Blood Ape stood between them and the river. It continued to pound its chest and roar its defiance, working itself up for a charge.

Mack and Pepsy raised their machetes and tensed.

"I've got this," Bones said. He was in survival mode now. His cryptid hunter instincts, the one that preferred flight over fight when encountering a previously unknown species, had been completely shut off. It was time to go to war.

The Blood Ape was a ferocious enemy, but its nature made it vulnerable. Rather than be intimated by the ape's display of aggression, Bones seized the opportunity to attack. He had nine bullets remaining in his magazine. He pumped three slugs into the beast's gut before it even realized it had been hit. His rising line of fire sent a slug into the muscular chest, another slicing along the side of its neck, and a third glancing off its skull.

Now the ape charged. Bones fired his three remaining bullets then let the Glock fall to the ground. He drew his Recon knife and made a mad dash toward the charging ape. At the last second, he dropped into a feet first slide. Like a baserunner evading a tag, he skidded past the injured creature's clumsy, grasping hands. He let out a yell and drove his knife into its chest. He felt it sink into the muscular chest, heard the beast let out a cry of pain.

The ape lurched forward, and Bones found himself lying on his back, looking up at the jungle foliage. Raindrops struck him in the face, cold and heavy. He sprang to his feet and drew his machete.

The knife had not done the trick, but the Blood Ape was

suffering the effects of the bullet wounds. It stumbled toward Mack and Pepsy, slipping on the wet path, shrieking in rage.

Bones attacked from behind. He swung the machete with all his might. It sliced deeply into the back of the ape's leg just above its right heel. Bones didn't know if the thing even had an Achilles tendon, but the blow did the trick. The ape stumbled and fell, then regained its feet.

Bellowing with rage and clutching its wounded stomach, the ape crashed away into the jungle.

Mack handed Bones his Glock, but his magazines were empty, and he had no time to reload them at the moment. He holstered the weapon and they plunged along the path.

The rain fell harder now, and the earth beneath their feet grew slick and muddy. They slipped, skidded, and stumbled their way down a steep slope and found themselves at the river's edge. With the storm rolling in, the water level was rising and the river churning.

They headed downriver, keeping close to the water's edge. In the distance, they could still hear the cries of the Blood Apes. Forked lightning struck the treetops nearby. The thunder hammered their eardrums. The rain was coming in sheets.

At least it will cover our scent, Bones thought.

"You've already implemented Plan B," Mack said. "Is there a Plan C?"

"Absolutely," Bones said. "There's no time to build a raft, so we're going to take Igor's riverboat."

"Are we sure that thing will float?" Mack asked.

Bones shrugged. "We'll know soon enough."

As they continued to work their way along the riverbank, Mack enumerated the reasons Bones plan wouldn't work: *Anastasia* might not be seaworthy, the engine probably didn't run, there wasn't a great deal of fuel in the hold, and how were they going to get the boat off of the riverbank and into the water?

Finally, Bones held up a hand to forestall her complaints. "No one's going to force you to get onto the boat. You can hike it or swim for it for all I care."

"I'm not saying I don't want to try it," Mack replied. "I just want to make sure you've thought of everything."

They spotted the old riverboat up ahead. The river had overflowed its banks and was now washing over the log platform upon which *Anastasia* rested. Bones could see that the platform was built on a gentle decline with the bow of the boat facing toward the water. The platform was held in place by three large stakes on the bottom end.

He grinned. Igor had known exactly what he was doing. The logs were rollers. Loose the mooring lines, pull the stakes free, apply a little muscle and the boat would roll down into the river. Even if they couldn't get the engine started, as long as the craft floated, the current would carry them away.

No sooner had the thought crossed his mind than the center stake broke free and *Anastasia* shifted forward. The force of the rising river was beginning to wash the platform away!

"Pick up the pace!" Bones shouted. That was no easy task. They were now slogging through fast-moving water that was halfway up Mack's calves and rising.

They reached the stern of the craft and Bones half boosted, half threw Mack over the gunwale. She turned to offer a hand up to Pepsy. Their fingertips touched and then Mack let out a cry of surprise as the boat pivoted hard to starboard. Another stake had broken free and the platform on which *Anastasia* rested was falling apart. It was only a matter of seconds now.

"Grab on to something!" Bones shouted as the platform gave way beneath them.

Anastasia shot forward and then lurched to a stop when she reached the end of her mooring ropes. Pepsy sloshed his way over to the stern. He took off his backpack, tossed it into the boat, and then began to climb in. With a loud crack, the stern side mooring rope snapped under the burden of his added weight. With a yelp of surprise, the guide lost his grip and plunged into the water.

"Pepsy!" Bones shouted. There was nothing he could do. As he struggled to reach the boat, the last mooring rope broke free. *Anastasia* shot forward. Her bow struck the last stake that was holding the platform in place. It broke free and the structure came apart. The earth seemed to fly out from underneath him. Seconds later, Bones found himself flat on his back, being carried along by the raging river. He caught a glimpse of charcoal gray sky, and then he was plunged beneath the depths.

25

Mack clutched *Anastasia's* port rail with one hand and the canopy with the other, steadying herself as the old riverboat plunged down the raging river. She squinted and tried to see through the torrential downpour.

Neither Bonebrake nor Pepsy had made it onto the boat. Where were they?

"Miss Red!" a voice called.

"Pepsy? Where are you?" She couldn't see him, but he sounded like he was close by. "Call out to me!"

A gurgling sound was his only reply. Lightning flashed and she saw Pepsy's head bobbing in the frothy river. Still clutching the rail, she extended her arm, but she couldn't quite reach him.

Anastasia was suddenly jostled to starboard as she struck something unseen. Probably a boulder. Mack fell hard to the deck, tasted blood in her mouth. But a split lip was nothing when your friends were dying.

She managed to get up onto her knees and shrug out of her heavy backpack. She dropped it onto the deck and crawled back toward the stern.

"Bonebrake! Pepsy!" she called out.

She heard Pepsy shout something unintelligible. Nothing from Bonebrake. She told herself he was all right. The man was indestructible.

The deck rose and fell with each swell of the river. Mack managed to regain her feet and look around. Pepsy was still floating off the port side, swept along by the raging torrent. He was managing to keep his head above water, but he appeared exhausted. He was even farther away than before. She needed to get to him before they were swept apart, or before he was dashed against one of the many boulders around which the frothy waters churned.

She spotted two long, wooden paddles lying on the deck. She snatched one up, leaned over the gunwale, and stretched out.

"Pepsy! Grab hold!"

Pepsy reached out and managed to catch the flat of the paddle between his thumb and forefinger. He held on for a second, then lost his grip.

Mack knew she had to find a way to extend her reach. Holding the paddle in her right hand and clinging to the canopy post with her left, she straddled the gunwale and leaned out toward Pepsy. *Anastasia* tilted wildly to port and Mack found her leg suddenly plunged underwater up to the knee.

"Can you reach it?" she shouted.

"Yes, Miss Red!" Pepsy seized the paddle in both hands. Mack held on with all her might and pulled.

It was like hauling a pile of wet blankets. Pepsy was heavy and the river pulled him down. She put everything she had into the attempt. Fire burst through her shoulder. It felt as if it would tear out of its socket, but she held on.

"Try to swim!" she shouted to Pepsy. "I can't do it on my own."

Pepsy kicked his legs furiously. Little by little, he inched closer to the boat. The rain was coming down in sheets and Mack felt her grip on the canopy post slipping.

"Not now," she said. "Almost got him."

Another bolt of lightning etched the image of Pepsy, almost within arm's reach, in her mind. And then *Anastasia* lurched. Mack lost her grip on the paddle and the rail. With a shout of surprise, she slipped to the side. She narrowly avoided a plunge into the river by hooking her left leg around the canopy post. She hung there for a moment, perpendicular to the gunwale. Then she heard a warning shout. She looked to her left and saw a massive boulder jutting up from the churning river.

It was a good thing she kept in shape because without all those crunches, she'd have never gotten her body into an upright position in time to keep her skull from being crushed like an egg. *Anastasia* swept past the boulder with inches to spare. Out of the corner of her eye, she spotted Pepsy, who was now using the paddle as a flotation device. One end of the paddle struck the boulder. Pepsy held on, but the impact sent him spinning.

"Dammit!" Mack shouted as he fell farther behind the riverboat.

"I got him!" a voice shouted.

Mack rushed to the stern and peered out into the storm. Bonebrake clung to the remains of a mooring rope. As *Anastasia* swept him forward past Pepsy, he reached out and caught hold of the guide. With a powerful heave, Bonebrake dragged Pepsy over to him. Pepsy seized the mooring rope and held on for dear life.

Mack could see that the pair were exhausted. She had to do something to help. She took hold of the mooring rope, braced her foot against the stern, and heaved. Bit by bit, hand over hand, she pulled the tired men closer to the boat. Finally, something was going right.

With a loud shriek, *Anastasia* suddenly ground to a stop. Mack was hurled backward with such force that she bounced once and slammed into the boiler. The breath left her in a rush, and she rolled over onto her back. She struggled to get back to her feet, to even take a breath, but pain and exhaustion kept frozen in place.

Damn! I almost had them.

And then two hands, one dark brown, one light brown, appeared over the lip of the stern rail. If she could have laughed, she would have. Bonebrake and Pepsy, looking like drowned rats, slowly hauled themselves onto the boat.

The three of them lay on the deck catching their breath until Pepsy finally spoke. "Mister Bone save my life."

Mack sat up fast, sending bolts of pain through her bruised ribs. She had nearly drowned trying to save the ungrateful jerk.

"What about me?" she asked.

"Mister Bone save you too? I did not see."

Mack closed her eyes and barked a rueful laugh. Typical men.

"Thanks for the assist, Red," Bones said. "It was all we could do to hang on."

"You're welcome." She almost smiled, but she was too weary. "I suppose we should see what this old tub is stuck on."

"I'll see if the hull has been breached," Bones said. Holding on to the rail, he managed to haul himself to his feet. Suddenly, he froze. He cocked his head and frowned as if listening intently.

"Hell freaking no," he muttered.

"What is it?" Mack asked, heart racing.

"Can you hear that?" Bones asked.

Mack concentrated. She tried to tune out the roar of the river, the creak of the boat as she shifted and swayed, the roll of thunder. And then she heard it. It sounded like an avalanche coming their way.

The three of them moved to the stern rail and gazed upriver, listening as the roar came closer. Lightning crackled, giving them a brief glimpse of a roiling wall of white water tumbling its way toward them. There was something hypnotically terrifying about it. It was pure, irresistible nature. And it was about to come crashing down on them.

26

Bones let out a curse as the wall of water rolled forward. It reminded him of the scene in one of the Lord of the Rings movies where the river turned into water horses and swept the villains away. He frowned. Why was he thinking about nerd stuff at a time like this?

"What's with that look on your face?" Mack asked.

"I suddenly have sympathy for the Nazgul."

Mack gaped for a full two seconds. "Nerd!" she shouted.

"My friend told me smart girls like those movies. It was research." Bones was never going to listen to Corey again.

"Does your vast knowledge of nerd culture include what to do in situations like this?" Mack asked.

Bones rolled his eyes. She wasn't going to let the nerd thing go.

"Just find something to hold on to and hope for the best. If you get thrown into the river, try and float on your back with your feet facing downstream so you don't bash your head against a rock."

Mack gave a resolute nod. There was something about giving instructions that instilled people with confidence. Just knowing that there was any form of plan gave people an illusion of control.

Bones quickly hauled in the rope that had saved his life. They took turns looping it around one wrist. Then they knelt by the stern and waited.

The rain had slackened, and the sky turned a lighter shade of gray, giving them a batter view of the latest thing that was going to try and kill them. The storm had dumped massive amounts of water into the many small tributaries that fed this branch of the river. The many had now converged into one, their concentrated fury bottled up in this single channel of the world's deadliest river.

Bones felt the river begin to rise again. And the ship

began to inch forward. If they could get moving before the surge struck, maybe they could ride this out. *Anastasia* shifted again. She was trying to break free, but they were almost out of time.

"Everybody grab your gear and get your asses forward." He pointed toward the bow in case Pepsy didn't completely understand. The pair obeyed immediately. Bones grabbed a paddle and followed behind. As they move forward, he felt the old boat shift again. Could it work?

"I want all our weight in the bow. Whatever we're snagged on, we're nearly free."

They reached the bow, and everyone threw their weight forward. The felt the stern rise, heard a scraping sound as *Anastasia* skidded forward. Bones ran toward the sound and saw that a small portion of the hull rested atop a flat rock. Bones set the paddle against the front of the rock and heaved. With a shriek of metal, the boat broke free and was once again being swept downriver at a rapid clip.

Mack and Pepsy let out a ragged cheer that died out as they felt the onrushing surge lift *Anastasia* higher and higher. The wall of water was almost as high as the canopy that covered *Anastasia's* stern deck. Bones hit the deck but didn't close his eyes.

Anastasia's stern was lifted high into the air. Bones slid along the rain-drenched deck and slammed into Mack, who in turn crushed Pepsy against the bow.

"Oh my God!" Mack yelled as the boat tilted forward. For a moment it felt as if *Anastasia* were standing on her nose. The three adventurers clung to one another as the riverboat plunged forward. Icy water washed over them as the bow was driven beneath the surface of the river. The sturdy craft bobbed right back up and kept going. She had taken on some water, but she was still afloat.

"Igor did a good job on the old girl!" Bones said. They were riding the crest of the surge now, swept along at an ungodly speed.

"Do you think she'll hold together?" Mack asked.

"You are so negative," Bones said. "Try to think positive for once."

Mack laughed, but her moment of mirth ended in a gasp. "I'm positive," she said, her voice trembling, "that's a waterfall up ahead."

There was no time to do anything but brace themselves before the old boat was flying through a cloud of mist. Bones felt the sensation of falling. How far was the drop-off?

They struck the water moments later. Once again, they were flung to the deck. Water poured in over the bow. Bones felt himself being washed back toward the stern. *Anastasia* was riding low in the water but miraculously, it remained afloat.

Bones rolled over onto his back and stared up at a sliver of blue sky that had appeared between the clouds. He was battered, bruised, and exhausted. But he was still alive.

"I don't want to stand," Mack said. "I'm afraid of seeing what's around the next bend."

"Worst is over," Pepsy said. The series of narrow escapes seemed to have invigorated him. "We check boat?"

Bones nodded and slowly got to his feet. He wanted to lie on the deck for a while longer, but they needed to assess *Anastasia's* condition. A quick inspection revealed no leaks, and the rudder was intact. He found a few buckets below decks, and he and Mack spent time bailing water while Pepsy manned the rudder.

Though the river had calmed, it was still running high and carrying them along at high speed. With any luck, they would make it back to civilization much quicker than it had taken them to hike in.

Finally, the water was bailed out, and the river was riding just high enough to carry the boat over most of the obstacles they would ordinarily have to navigate around. The skies had cleared and now the bright sun beat down on them, but there were no Blood Apes chasing them and no dangerous storms threatening to sink them.

While Bonebrake inspected the boiler and engine, Mack took time to once again thumb through Igor's journal. One day she would get the entirety of it translated. For now, she would settle for figuring out exactly where they were. That wouldn't be easy. Their escape was a blur in her memory. She had no idea what twists and turns they had taken as they were swept along by the raging river. Still, it was worth a try. She took a map from her backpack and started searching for landmarks that might correspond to places in Igor's journal.

By the time Bonebrake emerged from below decks and declared the steam engine "probably might work," she had gotten nowhere. She closed the journal and let out a sigh.

"I thought that would be good news," Bones said.

"Oh, sure. 'Probably might' always instills me with such confidence."

Bones shook his head and began firing up the boiler. Mack sat in sullen contemplation of the inscrutable map. Finally, the engine sputtered to life. The deck began to vibrate. Pepsy let out a whoop.

"Not much faster, but better to steer," he said.

"Good job, Bonebrake," Mack said. "I can't believe this thing runs."

"Igor deserves the credit. This boat must have been a labor of love for him." He sat down beside her and glanced at the map and journal. "What are we working on?"

"I was trying to pinpoint our location, but Igor's river map doesn't include many landmarks."

"Did you ask Pepsy if he knows where we are?"

Mack felt her cheeks grow hot. "Excuse me for a moment." Mustering all the dignity she could, she sidled over to Pepsy and held the map out in front of him. "Do you have any idea where we are?"

He frowned, looked at the map, then looked at the horizon. He did this twice more, then tapped a spot on the map.

"You're certain?" Mack asked.

He nodded.

Mack felt a chill pass over her. She hurried back, grabbed, the journal, and began flipping through the pages. Bonebrake raised his eyebrows but didn't ask what she was up to. She double-checked the journal, then another map on which Bonebrake had been keeping notes. She was right!

"I figured out where we are." She glared at him, daring him to correct her.

"You don't seem happy about it."

"It's probably nothing. It's just…"

An ear-splitting roar caused her to jump. She ran to the bow, already knowing what she would see. A dinosaur with a crocodilian head and a large fin on its back, came crashing out of the jungle up ahead. It stopped at the river's edge and bellowed.

"It's just that we're very close to the place where we met the Spinosaurus," Mack finished.

27

Even at a distance, the Spinosaurus was a terrifying sight. It stamped its feet and roared. The sound sent a shiver down Bones' spine. He had his Glock, two magazines, and a machete against one of the deadliest predators in history.

"Can we run?" Mack asked.

"Probably not. That thing can swim faster than *Anastasia* can move."

"I don't suppose it will let us pass on by," Mack said.

As if in reply, the Spinosaurus began moving in their direction. It was definitely locked in on them.

Bones had only one idea. "Take us over to the opposite bank, and tie us off, but be ready to launch when I give the word," Bones said to Pepsy. Their guide nodded, sweat rolling down his face, and steered *Anastasia* toward the south bank.

"What are you doing?" Mack asked.

"Buying us some time while I implement Plan C."

"I'm not even going to ask," she said.

"Just keep an eye on the dinosaur and let me know if it makes any sudden movements." Bones still wore Igor's stone whistle around his neck. Wouldn't hurt to try. He pressed the whistle to his lips and blew.

The whistle had no effect on the Spinosaurus. It continued to move along the bank a few steps at a time, stalking them. It stopped frequently to slap the water with its tail, or to let out one of its bloodcurdling roars. Bones blew again and again, to no effect. The dinosaur kept moving toward them.

"That worked well," Mack said. "What was your plan? Entice it to attack?"

"It drove Mokele-mbembe half-mad. I thought maybe we could entice it into a reckless charge and then slip past it?"

"Let me try." Mack took the whistle from him and blew. Nothing.

"Okay, here's what we're going to do," Bones said, easing his Glock from the holster. "As soon as Prickly Pete over there hits the water, we'll make a run for it. Keep the boat as close to shore as you can in case we have to abandon ship in a hurry. If that happens, you two keep going downriver while I work my usual magic."

"That sounds a lot like Plan B," Mack said.

Bones shrugged. "I keep things simple."

The Spinosaurus let out another roar and took a step into the water. Pepsy cut the single mooring rope and *Anastasia* lurched forward. The steam engine gave them a boost, but it was precious little. The dinosaur bellowed again.

"Will you shut up!" Mack shouted, then puffed on the stone whistle for emphasis.

A high-pitched cry resounded from somewhere in the jungle. Spinosaurus immediately turned around and answered the call. Another roar from the jungle, a little closer this time. Bones knew that sound well. The damn thing had nearly killed him.

"Keep blowing the whistle," he said to Mack, but she was already puffing away as if she were blowing up a balloon.

Mokele-mbembe answered again with its shrill cry, and Spinosaurus waded out of the river to meet her. Bones could see the treetops sway as the dinosaur crashed through the jungle.

"What do I do Mister Bone?" Pepsy asked.

"Just keep the throttle open and the bow pointed downriver," Bones said. "And pray to whichever gods you're into."

Pepsy nodded and began muttering a prayer. The boat

was now level with Spinosaurus, which stood on the opposite bank, waiting for Mokele-mbembe.

"Don't pay us any mind," Bones whispered as *Anastasia* puttered along.

No such luck. Spinosaurus suddenly remembered its original target. It turned and moved back into the water.

"Oh, hell no!" Bones shouted. He raised his Glock, took aim, and squeezed off a shot. The bullet glanced off the beast's head. It let out an angry hiss. Bones fired again, hoping for a miracle. Once again, the bullet met tough hide.

And then the trees on the opposite side of the river buckled as Mokele-mbembe came barreling out of the jungle. Spinosaurus turned and met her halfway.

Mokele-mbembe met the predator's charge with a vicious slap of her tail that caught it on one of its oddly bowed legs. Spinosaurus stumbled but recovered quickly and charged again.

The two massive beasts met at the river's edge. Mokele-mbembe was the larger of the two, and she drove her enemy back down into the water. Again and again, Spinosaurus tried to snap its jaws closed on the larger dinosaur's throat, but Mokele-mbembe kept the beast at bay and punished it again and again with its powerful tail.

Bones heard a faint click. Mack had taken out her camera and was snapping photographs. He couldn't help but laugh.

"I cannot believe what I'm seeing," she said.

"It's like something out of a movie," Bones agreed.

The two dinosaurs seemed to grow smaller as the boat bobbed down the river putting more distance between the adventurers and the prehistoric beasts. The rays of the setting sun bathed the combatants in blood-red light. Spinosaurus snapped and clawed, Mokele-mbembe smashed. The battle raged on long after they had rounded a bend and left the beasts behind.

"I don't care what you two say," Mack began, holding up

the stone whistle. "I'm taking credit for saving us."

Bones threw back his head and laughed. "That is just fine by me."

28

Bones would not have been at all surprised if they had returned to Pepsy's village of Kitoko to find King Kong himself at the gates. To his utter surprise, they made it back to the village the following day without encountering further difficulty. When they finally landed, Bones wanted nothing more than a quiet place to sleep for a few days. Preferably one free of dinosaurs and murderous apes.

They caused quite a stir when they brought Pepsy home safely with him at the helm of a much more interesting boat than the one in which he had left. The guide had been more than happy to take *Anastasia* in recompense for his boat that had been destroyed by the hippos. He was certain it would make him the most popular guide in the region. Bones doubted there were many competitors for that title.

After receiving treatment for his wounds, Bones slept the afternoon away. He woke to find Mack in his hut, once again looking through Igor's journal.

"That must be interesting reading," Bones said.

She smiled. "I translated his theories about the history of Mbanza Mpimpá. Well, I decoded them. The jerk got cute and wrote this part in a cipher."

"Let's hear it," Bones said.

"His theories pretty much match our own, and many of them are supported by fragments of myths and legends he collected from various tribes. He believes the city was built over a long period of time by some of the earliest inhabitants of the region as a place of worship and sacrifice. They realized the deadly nature of the meteorite, which they believed to be supernatural and sealed it away with the gold found in the crater.

"The Blood Apes were a particularly vicious, isolated group of apes. Due to their violent nature, which might have resulted from living so close to the exposed meteorite, the locals chose them to be used as sacrifices. The Noble Apes kept to themselves and were left alone. Eventually, the Blood Apes broke free. They slaughtered the locals, imitating the ritual sacrifice they had learned from their human captors."

"Funny how that works," Bones said.

Mack nodded. "Eventually, the city was forgotten as were the unique apes that called the city and the surrounding area home. With its remote location, all the natural dangers, plus dinosaurs, it was easy for the location to remain off the radar."

"Until Igor found it," Bones said.

"Funny thing. He discovered the boat first. He made many treks out into the jungle to work on her, never knowing he was so close to the city."

"I guess the Blood Apes frightened him away for good," Bones said.

"Why did he try and get us killed? Mack asked. "Why not simply refuse to lead us to Mbanza Mpimpá?"

"We had the GPS coordinates. He knew we would find the city sooner or later. And I'm not sure he wanted to kill us. Probably hoped an encounter with a living dinosaur would put a scare into us."

Mack nodded. "Most journalists would be happy to get out of the jungle with their lives and photographic evidence of Mokele-mbembe. I'm more stubborn."

"You did good," Bones said.

"Thanks. I'd say the same to you, but this is kind of what you do, right?"

He laughed but nodded. "Yep, this is me."

"Some life…"

He shrugged. "It has its good moments too."

"And bad ones."

He sighed. "Too many sometimes."

Turning, he held out his hand, but Mack threw her arms around him and squeezed him tight. Tears streaked down her face. There was no intimacy in the embrace. It was an expression of companionship, a deep bond shared by people who had faced death together and lived to tell the tale. He wrapped his arms around her, feeling uncomfortable for a moment. He liked Mack, but not in that kind of way. She was tough and resilient, and she had earned his respect. Like Nico back in Cabras, Bones might have just found another ally he could count on.

"I have a confession to make," Mack said, suddenly shoving him away. She grabbed her backpack, opened it, and set it down in front of him. It made a heavy clunk when it struck the earthen floor. "I took quite a bit of gold from the temple. It's only right that I share it with you."

Bones looked at the gold and laughed. "No wonder you were so slow climbing out of the canyon."

"At least I didn't have to be carried out. Besides, Pepsy took as much gold as I did."

"Fair enough," Bones said. "Since we're playing true confessions, I snagged a couple handfuls myself." He patted his pockets. "I regretted it while I was hanging on to the mooring rope and trying to keep my head above water."

Mack shook her head. "I should have known. I don't suppose you can help me get this out of the country? No offense, but you seem like you might know people."

"I know people who know people," Bones said. "We can get it converted to cash the money sent to us in a way that can't be traced."

"What will it cost us?" Mack asked.

"The deal is for twenty percent. It'll probably end up being half before it's all said and done. It will still be a lot of money. And you're about to become the most famous journalist in the world."

"I suppose I'll have my fifteen minutes," she said. "But is

it worth it? Regardless of what I said to Igor, I don't see this ending well for any of those creatures."

"You're going to kill the story?" Bones asked, surprised.

"I think I can rewrite this as a travel piece. The villages we visited, the discovery of *Anastasia*, our escape, the storm. That will make for an interesting piece and I've got plenty of photographs to go with it. But I haven't made up my mind."

"Whatever you decide, if there's any way to leave my name out of it, I'd be grateful," Bones said. "I like the fortune but not the glory."

"I'll see what I can do," Mack said.

Just then, a familiar face appeared in the doorway of the hut. It was Pepsy.

"Mister Bone! I tell everyone how you save me. How you lead me to treasure and give me a fine boat. We hold a feast in your honor."

With each word, Mack's face grew redder. She tried to say something, but all she managed were angry stammers.

"You heard him, Red. There's going to be a feast to honor the hero of the day. Are you coming?"

"I suppose," she said darkly.

The two followed Pepsy out of the hut and into the village. Bones closed his eyes and breathed in the aroma of roasted meat. His stomach growled. How long had it been since he'd had a hearty meal? His thoughts were interrupted when Mack took him by the hand.

She gazed into his eyes, then reached out and touched his cheek.

"Thank you for everything, Bones."

He smiled. "You're welcome, Mackenzie."

The End

ABOUT THE AUTHORS

David Wood is the USA Today bestselling author of the action-adventure series, The Dane Maddock Adventures, and many other works. He also writes fantasy under his David Debord pen name. When not writing, he hosts the Wood on Words podcast. David and his family live in Santa Fe, New Mexico. Visit him online at davidwoodweb.com.

Matt James is the critically acclaimed author of eight titles, including *Blood & Sand*, *Mayan Darkness*, *Babel Found*, *Elixir of Life*, *Plague*, *Evolve*, *Dead Moon*, and now, *Berserk*. He lives in West Palm Beach, Florida with his family. You can visit him at:
www.Facebook.com/MatthewJamesAuthor
www.JamestownBooks.Wordpress.com
Instagram: MatthewJames_Author
Twitter: @MJames_Books

Manufactured by Amazon.ca
Bolton, ON